I0718137

The Rock Star's Email Order Bride

DEMELZA CARLTON

Book 2 in the Romance Island Resort series

DEDICATION

For the real Magic Marcel.

ONE

Jason didn't wait for the rotors to stop before he leaped out of the helicopter door and sprinted for the hotel entrance.

"Welcome to Romance Island Resort, sir. Enjoy your stay!" came the pilot's voice behind him, but Jason wasn't listening.

He burst through the door and skidded to a stop in front of the Reception desk. "Where's Audra?" Jason demanded. She was the only girl who could make him forget Angel. The only girl who could make this right. He needed her. Now.

The blonde girl at Reception stared at him. "We don't have anyone named Audra here, sir."

"Of course you do. Best maid I ever met. Tell her I'm here, and to meet me at my accommodation. I had Villa Maxima last time. The one with the huge spa tub in the bathroom. And make sure we have plenty of mango beer. Mangoes are her favourite."

A second girl sidled behind the desk, beside to the

blonde. She looked Japanese, but her accent had Aussie overtones as she asked, "Did you say Audra? She was mad about mangoes. I bet Audra's missing those now she's in Antarctica."

Jason laughed. "Antarctica? Don't be ridiculous." He turned his eyes back to the blonde. "Can you let her know I'm here?"

She looked lost until her eyes fixed on someone behind Jason. "Oh, Mr Meier, this man's looking for Audra. He doesn't believe that she's gone."

An older man with a professional smile held out his hand. "Good morning, Mr ah – "

"Felix. Jason Felix." Jason's firm handshake almost crushed the other man's fingers in his eagerness. "Where's Audra?"

"Like Hana said, she's in Antarctica, Mr Felix. Audra no longer works here."

Jason's heart plummeted. No Angel, no Audra...what was a rock star supposed to do when the girl he wanted didn't want him?

"Is there anything else we can help you with, Mr Felix?" the blonde asked sweetly.

Find another girl.

He eyed the blonde, who wore a pink and white frangipani behind her ear that matched her pink lips. "Make one of the villas ready for me."

She looked askance at Meier.

Meier coughed and dropped his voice to a carrying whisper, "Mr Felix owns the hotel, Heloise. Give him anything he wants."

Heloise beamed. "Sure thing, Mr Felix. What else would

you like?"

"I'm the activities manager, Mr Felix," Hana interjected. "My job is to make sure every guest enjoys his holiday to the fullest. Tell me what you want, and I'll make it happen."

His loins stirred at the thought. Who first — the blonde or the brunette?

"Stand up," Jason ordered. "Both of you."

Heloise rose and Jason eyed her breasts. More than a handful — much too big for his tastes. Maybe some other time. He turned to scrutinise the brunette instead. Jason took stock of her athletic figure, perky breasts and rosebud mouth. She'd definitely do for a night.

"Join me for a drink. I'd like to tell you what activities I have in mind." He crooked his finger and headed for the bar, grinning when he heard Hana's following footsteps. Yes, he was still a rock star. No woman could resist him.

TWO

"I'm sending you to Australia," Phuong's father had told her. "There you can study accounting until you're qualified. A proper CPA. Then you will come home to sort out my company. You'll check all my accounts and find out who's stealing from me. I suspect my accountant, Felipe, but he's family – your brother's wife's brother – and your brother swears he's honest, so we need proof before we can fire Felipe and give you his job. So study hard, because this family's fortunes rest on you."

"Why me? Why not Thuan?" Phuong asked.

He sighed. "Because you're ten times as clever as your brother, who's also blinded by love for the stupid woman he calls his wife. She'll spend all his money and leave him when he's bankrupt to marry some other stupid man. You'll never be seduced by a pair of batting eyelashes over a dissatisfied pout. Love won't make a fool of you."

He was right, Phuong reflected. If she was ever foolish enough to fall in love, her mother's acid comments would soon dissuade her of any such sentimental feeling.

Sadly, her father's plans hadn't come to fruition in his lifetime. A stroke felled him in his sleep, leaving her brother in charge of both the business and the family finances.

Her brother's phone call had been abrupt. "I'm not wasting any more money on you. Felipe tells me Dad's business is nearly bankrupt, so we have to cut all unnecessary expenses – including educating you. I don't know what Dad was thinking," Thuan said, without even greeting her.

"But I only have a year to go. Then I'll be able to work for Dad's firm and turn the company around, just like he wanted," Phuong protested. "Just one more year."

"Not one more cent," he snapped. "There's no point educating girls. Look at my wife, Pearl. You might work for a few years, but then you'll get married and have children – what do you need an education for, when all you'll do is cooking, cleaning and childcare? And I won't support you any more, either. Pearl says we can barely afford to support Mother and we have nothing left to waste on you. You're too old. Find a job or a husband. You won't be welcome here." Before Phuong could respond, he'd hung up. That would be the last time she'd speak to her brother.

Find a job or a husband. Her Australian visa didn't allow her to work more than ten hours a week, which was hardly enough to pay for her final year of university fees. It would barely cover her food for the week, let alone her rent. She knew what she had to do – find a husband, and fast. An Australian man who could give her Australian citizenship.

Then she could finish her degree and save her father's firm. If Felipe and her brother hadn't bankrupted it already.

A husband. She needed a husband. Where did a girl go to get a husband quickly? The internet, of course. She knew other girls back home who'd been mail-order brides and they'd raved about the experience. The men had romanced their brides-to-be, whisked them away to their home countries, married them and given them a future. She also knew girls back home who'd done worse – sold their bodies to many men, not just one, in order to help the family finances. Compared to prostitution, marriage to a stranger couldn't be that bad – perhaps there'd be some handsome, charming, rich one who'd sweep her off her feet and into the lap of luxury. Then her brother would be begging her for favours.

Smiling to herself, Phuong opened her laptop. She had a husband to find.

THREE

"Hello? I need a fuck."

Xan blinked and forced her smile to stay in place. "I'm sorry, what did you say?"

"I need a fuck." The frustrated-looking backpacker glared at her. "And a plate."

Xan repeated the man's accented English several times in her head before she decided not to kick him in the groin for one of the coarsest come-on lines she'd ever been hit with. Instead, she replied, "Ah, you want a fork? It's a ten-dollar deposit to get a crockery and cutlery pack — one of everything you need, including a plate and a fork. Here, let me show you." Xan rose and retrieved one of the drawstring bags from the office. She tipped it on the counter, sending a cascade of cutlery across the desk.

"Ten…ten dollars for a fuck?"

She had to keep a straight face. She HAD to. Xan took a

deep, calming breath.

"Yes. It's a deposit. When you return this at the end of your stay, I'll give your ten dollars back." Xan watched the backpacker thinking it over. She could almost read his mind. Yes, ten dollars was cheap for what you got, but he didn't know if he could find the items cheaper in a discount store in town. If he did, he could return these and get his money back. But if he bought things, he'd never see that money back, even if he did get his ten dollars from her. He didn't have much space in his already overstuffed backpack because of all the souvenirs he wanted to take home. Maybe he'd just hand over the money and… Xan tried to hide her smile as he produced the cash. "Here you go." She bagged the cutlery and passed the pack across the counter.

Fresh off the plane, she was sure of it. If he'd stayed at any other hostels in Australia before coming to Broome, he'd know the drill by now. She watched him disappear through the swinging kitchen door, before he reappeared in a group of equally lost-looking girls by the communal refrigerator. He'd evidently been their spokesman, because the girls trooped out of the kitchen and laid siege to the reception desk.

Xan did a quick head count and retrieved enough packs for everyone. She needn't have hurried, though – the girls weren't familiar enough with Australian currency to produce a single ten-dollar-bill between them. She saw euros, ringgit and what looked like Thai baht surface, before they'd produced enough dollars to seal the deal.

By the time the crowd cleared, the airport shuttle arrived, bringing with it a group of even more lost-looking souls, panting like dogs in the unfamiliar heat as they hefted their suitcases up the steps. Everyone wanted to visit a tropical paradise, but no one wanted to stay outside in the heat for long. Especially not in wet season humidity.

"Excuse me, but where are the cups? I want to make a cup of tea, but I can't seem to find them." The wilting woman had arrived on yesterday's shuttle, but Xan had been serving in the kiosk at the time, so one of the other girls had handled check-in.

Xan explained about the packs and endured a ten-minute argument as to why the woman couldn't just pay for the cup. It was the whole pack or nothing. It took another five minutes for the woman to produce the money she grumpily acknowledged was necessary, though she tried to tell Xan she was two dollars short while hiding the stack of twenties nestled in her wallet.

A queue coughed and shuffled at the kiosk, but the two girls who took turns in the kitchen and manning the counter were nowhere to be seen. Sighing, Xan stepped up to the counter and proceeded to sell soft drinks, laundry detergent and anything that could be deep-fried to the impatient guests. When the queue cleared, she took the food orders into the kitchen, where she found her missing staff peering at one girl's phone.

"It sounds like a dream come true," the phone's owner breathed. What was the girl's name? Heather, that was it.

"I'd say it's more of a nightmare," Xan interjected as she slapped the orders on the counter. "All these people were waiting to be served, so hurry up and get the orders ready."

"No, look at it, Xan," Adele replied, pulling Heather's phone from her fingers and handing it to Xan. "Seriously, it's got to be the best job in Broome. Tours and activities coordinator for the luxury resort island the celebrities go to. They want you to be a dive master, fluent in at least two languages, and all sorts of things, though. And a degree! But you get paid to snorkel and dive and go on helicopter tours all day…and you get to live on that island all the time."

A luxury resort sure sounded better than watching backpackers count their pennies all day. Xan hadn't thought she was ready for children, but now it seemed like she had hundreds of them. All adult-sized and asking the same questions, over and over and over again. Her visa would expire at the end of the dry season, though, which meant she needed to return to the UK, her family and her fiancé. She missed Jerome like an ache in the…well, touring the world was one thing, but travelling celibate, knowing that he was counting on her coming home when he finished his studies so they could get married, get a house and do all the things newlyweds did? Sometimes it was enough to make her want to return early. Firmly stamp on what Jerome called her travel bug and settle down with him.

For a moment, she considered it.

A shrill scream broke through her reverie. Assuming the worst, Xan took the stairs two at a time to the source of the sound: the female communal bathrooms. Damn. Why couldn't it be the male ones?

"What's the problem?" she called as she strode in.

Cries of, "Kikker!" and "Katak!" echoed through the steam, followed by, "What's a fucking frog doing in here? Aaargh!"

Xan assumed her calm-the-mob tone. "Nothing to worry about. Just a frog. It can't hurt you. I'll get someone to catch it when we close the bathroom for cleaning in an hour. Welcome to Western Australia, where the wildlife's so friendly, it joins you in the shower!"

One of the frog's friends snorted, but no one said anything else, so Xan headed back downstairs to the reception desk.

"Frog?" Adele asked as she handed a customer his change across the kiosk counter.

"Frog."

No, she couldn't go home yet. She was having too much fun. She hoped the frog appeared in the men's bathrooms next, or one of the big bush spiders. It was shift change for the oil and gas platform workers tomorrow. Some of those guys were ripped.

Maybe she should apply for that island resort job. How many dive masters with tourism degrees would there be around here? This was the trip of a lifetime: one big blast before she settled down for good with Jerome. It should include a piece of paradise. Go big or go home, she decided. And she wasn't ready to go home yet. Even if her life was all forks with no fucks.

"Hi, I'm new here and I can't find any spoons in the kitchen." The nervous-looking girl stared pitifully at Xan. "Please, can you tell me where to find them?"

"There's a ten-dollar deposit," Xan began wearily.

FOUR

Audra had never been so exhausted in her life, so naturally, she wanted to dance on the ceiling. She wasn't sure how many people had actually seen the South Pole, but now she was one of them. It felt…exhilarating. Hence the need to dance as soon as she could shut the door of her tiny room, where no one would see. The buzzing in her blood was better than sex. Everyone had sex.

Except…her room wasn't hers. Well, it was, but it was someone else's too. The vacant bunk she'd considered her reading lounge was now occupied by a girl with a round, smiling face. "Hi, hi! Finally we meet. I'm Shelley! You must be Audra. The guys told me it's your first trip and you've already seen the pole. Three winters I've spent here and my first expedition out there, I failed the medical and you got to go instead."

"I'm sure there'll be others. Some of the equipment

wasn't up to spec, so when the right stuff arrives next summer, a team will need to return." Audra couldn't keep the longing out of her tone. Of course she wanted to be part of it. Who wouldn't? But she was only covering Shelley's maternity leave, after all, and it looked like her time was up. "How's your little girl, anyway?"

Now it was Shelley's turn to look wistful. "She said her first word the day before I left: Mum. It killed me to leave her, but Ross and I agreed that he'd get to be a stay-at-home dad with her while I went off to work. God, I hope he can handle it." She waved at their cramped room. "This'll seem like a holiday in comparison, though."

They both laughed.

"Sorry, you probably want a minute to yourself after all that time in the field. Video calls home and such. I'll go take a shower before the boys use all the water." Shelley grabbed her towel and slung it over her shoulder.

"Watch out for the shower monitor. He's a big Russian bloke named Boris. If you try to take a shower even a second longer than three minutes, he'll bust in and carry you off for torture and whatever else Russians do to traitors. Apparently."

Shelley's face fell. "You mean Bruce left? He's the best plumber on the continent!"

Audra couldn't hide her smile. "No, but he did spend a whole day booming at me in a thick Russian accent until one of the other guys ratted him out. I've never forgotten to time my showers since."

Shelley laughed and headed for the showers.

Alone, Audra decided dancing was probably a bad idea, so she dusted off her laptop and woke it up. Calling home could wait until tomorrow, but she could catch up on news and email in the meantime. Hundreds of unread emails awaited her, so she sighed and sat down to sort the spam from the…sixty-three emails from Jay? More?

Huh. She hadn't heard a peep from him since she left Romance Island, and she never expected to, either. Well…okay, for the first week she'd kind of hoped, and maybe for the second one, too, especially after she'd sent him the photo of them together, and the third week…but by the time she'd boarded the *Aurora Australis*, she'd barely checked her email at all. And not because of the restricted internet access, either.

So why on Earth was he sending her thrice-daily emails? Curiosity won and she opened the most recent one.

WHY WON'T YOU ANSWER MY MESSAGES?

Another:

WE WERE MADE FOR EACH OTHER. WHERE ARE YOU?

That popped up a lot, though the wording varied a bit, depending on the day.

After the first couple dozen, Audra skimmed to the first one he'd sent.

I'M HOME. WHERE ARE YOU, BABY? WHY AREN'T YOU HERE?

Had he completely forgotten about her new job? The reason she was leaving the island? Maybe he was drunk. It still didn't explain why he thought she should be at the resort.

Exasperated, Audra typed a response:

"I'm at Davis as one of the Antarctic meteorology team this summer. I just got back from an expedition to Dome

Argus and the South Pole. It was awesome, thanks for asking." She hit send and scrolled through her emails, looking for anything from her family and friends.

Her laptop chimed, signalling that someone wanted to start a video call. Jay, who else?

She hadn't had a shower in days and her hair had been mashed under an assortment of hats and hoods for weeks. One look at her would scare him off for life. Reluctantly, she allowed the call to connect.

"Where the fuck are you really?"

Jay Felix was all charm.

Audra took a deep breath. She'd thought the soundproofing at the resort was bad. Here at Davis, if she raised her voice, the whole building would hear. "Hi, Jay. It's lovely to see you again. It's been months, I'm sure, though I gather you've been busy with your band's tour. I've been very busy, too. First training for my first Antarctic expedition, and then living and working out here for the summer. There are real penguins here, not just a jetty named after one. I must say, the jetty smells better, though."

"Why aren't you here?" Judging by his slurred voice, sobriety had deserted him several hours ago.

"I don't work at Romance Island Resort any more, remember?"

"No. Was it because of me? Did you quit because of me? I told you I was coming back, babe. I own the hotel. Had to come back."

He hadn't known? Then what had he meant that night when they'd… "That last night we spent together. When you answered the door, you said I was just in time and I'd left it until the last minute. You knew it was my last day and I was flying out to Hobart on Monday."

"No, I fucking didn't. You never told me that!"

Audra mulled this over. "So let me get this straight. You spent the night with me, made all sorts of promises you had no intention of keeping, then flew out the next morning to record your new album and go on tour. All the while, not saying a single thing to me. Not a word, a phone call, an email, nothing, until now, when you're demanding to know why I'm not waiting for you with open arms after you deserted me?"

"I didn't desert you! I had to work!"

"And who doesn't? When I got offered the chance of a lifetime, a stint in Antarctica, I took it. I'd have been crazy not to. Especially after dealing with VIPs who threw tantrums, painted the walls with ketchup, and slept with anything in a skirt." She'd never get the image of Jay and Penny out of her mind. It would scar her for life.

"Ooh, is that your boyfriend? Hi, I'm Shelley, Audra's roommate." Shelley smiled and waved over Audra's shoulder before throwing herself on her bed. "Don't mind me."

"Yes, I'm Audra's – " Jay began.

Audra cut in, "No, he's not my boyfriend. Never was, never will be. He used to be my boss." Though it was on the tip of her tongue, she didn't add that he'd once been the bane of her existence. It didn't seem fair to kick a man when he was down.

"What about all the time we spent together?" Jay exploded. "Are you honestly saying everything – the time, the incredible sex – meant nothing to you?"

Audra heard Shelley laugh softly, then whisper an apology.

"It was one night, Jay. One night that you made astonishingly clear meant nothing to you, when you climbed into a helicopter the morning after, then ignored me for months while wrapping yourself in different girls every night. Do you even remember how many? I mean, you did twenty, thirty shows at least, and I know for a fact that you took half a dozen girls back to your hotel room after the Perth concert. Add that all up and I don't need to be a statistician to know you've probably slept with over a hundred women, while you didn't even have time to send me an email saying hi." She drew in a deep, shaky breath. "If it weren't for the other girls, maybe I'd be interested if we were to meet again. But right now, if you showed up in the snow outside my door, I'd kick you right back to the boat that brought your sorry arse to Antarctica."

His eyes got that kicked puppy look that a dog gets when…Audra had never kicked a puppy, but she figured hurt and betrayal and big, wide eyes would feature in there somewhere.

"But…I could fly there now. We can talk about this. I could take you home and…I want to spend the rest of my life with you. How about it? A fresh start with just you and me. I'll marry you if that's what you want. No other women ever again. I swear." That same beseeching look she'd surrendered to before. Never again.

"Jay, you barely know me. Normal people don't marry strangers. Especially not strangers who've slept with a hundred other people in less than six months!"

"Please, baby, give me time to book a flight and – "

Audra's heart nearly broke at the pain in his voice, but somehow she mentally sticky-taped it back together and said, "No. I ship out in a couple of days. Even if you did fly here, I'd be gone, on my way back to Melbourne to finish my training. I told you before, if you want a girl to love you, you have to be more than a rock star. Go back to the hotel library and do some more research. You'll see what happens to guys who cheat. They don't get the girl, that's for sure." She sighed. "I'm sure she's out there, Jay – the right girl for you. But I'm not her. So good night…and good luck." Before he could say anything, she ended the call and slammed her laptop closed.

Shelley whispered, "Was that really Jay Felix?"

Audra nodded.

"And you used to work for him?"

Another nod.

Shelley cleared her throat. "He's always had a reputation for…well, you know. But I've always wondered if it was true or just something the girls made up. What's he like in bed?" In alarm, she added, "I'm only asking in the name of scientific inquiry, of course. Happily married and stored in this fridge and all."

Audra smiled faintly. "Unbelievable."

Shelley inhaled sharply. "I knew it! Wait, in a good way or a bad way?"

"Both."

They both laughed, but Audra's heart wasn't in it any more.

Shelley was sensitive enough to stop. "He seems really into you, despite all his obvious failings. Is there any chance you and him might…you know…reconnect? In some way?"

Audra shook her head. "If he grew up a bit, and maybe turned into a good man instead of a spoiled, selfish arsehole…maybe. But I think hell will freeze over first." She glanced out the window and noticed snow flurrying past the glass, dancing in an evening breeze that she'd never grow tired of watching.

Unseen by anyone, her tears for Jay dropped onto the windowsill. One, two, three, four…the beats of a song that only her heart knew.

FIVE

Jay lost count of the number of times he tried to call Audra again after the first call disconnected, but he just couldn't reach her. He couldn't quite bring himself to believe it. One moment, he'd been thrilled to finally speak to her again, and the next, he was all at sea. She wanted to work in a frozen wasteland and she didn't want him? What was wrong with her?

He'd have to talk to her in person, that was all. He'd find a plane or charter one to take him out there and…

Two hours later, he'd managed to find a cargo plane leaving New Zealand in a fortnight's time that would take him. Too late, if Audra had been telling the truth, because she'd already be on the ship home. Maybe he could track her down in Melbourne, but he wouldn't know where to start looking. Besides, he wasn't a stalker – he stood out and was proud of it.

And who was Audra, anyway? Just a hotel maid turned weathergirl, who'd saved his life and helped him and…aw, fuck. He'd messed up again. Done something wrong and lost her for good this time. And there wasn't a thing he could do about it. At least, not yet.

He needed to work out what he'd done wrong, so it wouldn't happen again. Rock gods didn't get dumped – not even retired ones.

Time to head back to the library. He'd get as many books as he could carry, and this time he'd pay attention. He'd get this romance thing sorted so no woman could resist him. So when the right one came along…she'd be his, no question. And no fuck-ups.

The library was closed by the time he reached it, but he'd persuaded the security manager to give him access to more than what the regular guests got. He was the owner, after all. After-hours access to the library? Easy.

He headed straight for the shelf where the rock star romances were kept. No matter what Audra said, he'd gotten some of his best ideas from these. As if someone had been expecting him, he found three new ones he'd never seen before – recognisable because of the absence of shirtless dudes on the cover, of course. He checked the bit on the back and they seemed sufficiently similar to the shirtless books to suit him.

What else had she said? Something about marrying strangers. Those were the mail-order brides, weren't they? Funny, she'd admitted that she liked those books, and he'd even seen her reading a couple. He grabbed those, too, figuring they might help.

Five books should do him for a couple of days, he

decided, so he tucked them under his arm and left the library, whistling as he walked around the lagoon, back to his villa.

Three books and a lot of bourbon later, he discovered that he'd missed the first book in the series, so he staggered back there to find it. It figured — had a shirtless dude on the cover. No wonder he'd ignored it the first time. May as well get some more of the mail-order bride books, too, to cover up the shirtless dude.

He'd read it as soon as he got another bottle of bourbon. The last one had somehow emptied itself and he couldn't be fucked finding another one. Yeah. But now, he'd just rest his head on the rug for a moment. Because...because...

Jason's head touched the rug and he fell into a deep, whisky-soaked sleep where he was a rock star again, and everything was rosy. Fuck yeah.

SIX

All out of fucks and forks to give, Xan collapsed on her bed. Burying her face in her pillow, she tried to shut out the world, but she didn't have time for that yet. She had to call home.

Easing her phone out of her bag, she checked that the wi-fi was active and started a video call to her parents.

Her dad answered the call, peering blearily at the screen. Was it just Xan's imagination, or was his nose red? Surely he couldn't be drunk at – she checked her watch – ten in the morning. He rarely drank anything.

"Xanthe, is that you? You look so tanned."

"Hi, Dad. Yeah, it's hard not to get tanned out here. The backpackers I manage is pretty open to the elements and it's only a short walk to Cable Beach, when I get time. They call it the wet season here, but we get fewer rainy days than you probably see."

After chatting for a few minutes about life in Broome and some of the strange things Dad's English students had said lately, Xan felt it was safe to ask, "Where's Mum?"

"Trying to single-handedly cure the plague, or that's what she says. I caught the dreaded lurgy from someone at work so your mother's at the supermarket buying ingredients for soup." He sneezed, then finished with a hacking cough. "Impressive, eh?"

Only her father could dramatise dying of man-flu. "Very. You make me really glad I'm on the other side of the world and it's summer here." She tried again. "Just that Mum emailed me, saying she needed to talk to me. It sounded ominous. You wouldn't know what she meant, would you?"

Her father shrugged. "No idea. Maybe she just wants to give you the recipe for her plague-curing soup. It can't be that bad if I haven't heard anything, can it?"

Xan finally relaxed. "No, that's true. Maybe she wants me to send more Vegemite for your birthday."

Her father failed to hide his horror. "Oh God, please no. Don't send any more of that stuff. Do Aussies really eat that? How are any of them still alive?"

Xan laughed. "It's the best hangover cure ever, or so I've been told. I've never had so much to drink that I wanted to try it. Watching tourists try it for breakfast at the backpackers never gets old, though. Their expressions…no words are necessary."

"So you like working there, then? Thinking of extending your stay?"

"Maybe." Xan thought about leaving it at that, but she'd always told her father everything. "I saw a better job advertised at a luxury resort near here. Well, a couple hundred kilometres from here, actually, on an island. They're looking for someone to manage all the activities at the hotel. That includes diving and snorkelling – they've got some awesome coral reefs there that I'd kill to dive, but you can only get to them through the hotel because of the shape of the island. They cater to VIPs, so you have to factor in anything that's within reach of a helicopter, light plane or luxury yacht…and they have access to all three. The pay's good and it includes accommodation and board on the island, so I wouldn't have to share a house in town and pay rent, either."

"Sounds perfect for you. That's what you want, right? All that time at university studying tourism management. I know we talked about history tours of the Greek islands, but with the economy the way it is…maybe you're better working in paradise in Australia. Perhaps one day I can persuade your mother to come for a visit."

Xan breathed a sigh of relief. She'd been thinking it, but to hear it from her father broke through all her remaining resistance. "I'll put in my application tonight."

A few minutes later, she ended the call and switched on her laptop. Yes, she wanted to do more diving before she settled down to a dull, married existence.

SEVEN

Pounding began in Jason's head. It wasn't until he cracked one eye open that he realised there was pounding outside it, too. On the door. "Fuck off," he mumbled. He reached across the bed, but there was nothing to grab but linen. Where were all the girls? He remembered two, maybe three of them, but they weren't here now. That meant no one else would answer the door and the hammering wouldn't stop until he did something about it.

"Yeah, coming," he growled. He reached the front door and waved it open.

"Mail delivery, Mr Felix." The night porter waved at the box of fan mail, topped by a small stack of official-looking envelopes that he should probably read first.

Jason kicked the box inside and grinned when it skidded on the polished tiles, spilling the stack of bills across the floor. White envelopes, white tiles…and one matte black envelope with the address printed on a sparkly silver label. He picked it up and flipped it over, wondering who'd died. It's not like he got funeral invitations very often. Maybe it was one of the Stones or some other rock royalty, acknowledging him as heir apparent to the title of the King of Rock, and begging him to attend the funeral of their old frontman and take his place in the band.

He squinted at the address, struggling to focus on the ornate script. Miller. Who'd he know named Miller? At an address in Perth…

Shrugging, Jason ripped it open and a shower of black glitter floated to the floor. The embossed card in his hand was an invitation, all right. To the wedding of Dr Alana Angel Miller and…fuck! He threw it on the floor, wanting to stomp it into the tiles. Angel was marrying the crazed stalker? The psycho who'd nearly killed her, then tried to beat Jason up, too, when he came to visit her in hospital?

Ignoring his splitting headache, he marched to find his phone. Without hesitating, he punched his sister's number and leaned against the kitchen bench while the call trilled for her to answer.

Pick up, pick up, pick up…she had to.

"Hi Jason. This really isn't a good time. I'm – "

"What the fuck is this? Is she fucking crazy?" he interrupted. "He should be locked up and not allowed near her. She should be committed to a mental hospital. Fucking insane…"

"Right, one second. I told my boss it's a family emergency and, seeing as the whole room heard you, I think he'll believe anything, provided I get your profanity the hell out of his meeting. I take it you got the invitation?" The faint sound of a door closing came down the phone line. "Okay, Jason. I'm back in my office and I've closed the door so everyone in the building doesn't have to listen to you swearing. She said she wanted to invite you and I gave her your address."

Then she knew he hadn't left the state. She knew where he was. Fuck, did that mean tomorrow she'd be on his doorstep, knife in hand?

"She said she'd castrate me, Jo! Cut my fucking balls off. What part of that didn't you believe? You're the one who keeps telling me to stay away from her. She carries that knife with her everywhere. And you told her where I live?" Shouting hurt his head, but he couldn't seem to turn down the volume on his own voice.

"She didn't really mean it," Jo soothed. "She was angry. You'd set some security guard to stalk her without telling her. You scared her."

"She wasn't fucking scared. Do you know what she did to the guy? Her and that steroid-enhanced psycho she thinks she's going to marry? She stabbed him. Fucking stabbed him. Then tied him up with electrical tape and tortured him until he told her everything. In her own apartment." Jay hadn't slept for three days after he'd heard that, certain he'd be next. If Angel didn't hunt him down, she'd send the psycho instead, and that guy liked inflicting pain. Just look at what he did to her. "She can't marry him. She just fucking can't!"

Jo sighed. "She can and she will, Jason. Look, I don't like him, either, but she can take care of herself. We're not teenagers any more. Even before Chaya made the charts, she had the money to hire security to watch her twenty-four seven. Trevor says he's not a threat and he'd know. He saw combat in Afghanistan, for God's sake. You're just jealous!"

"No, I'm not!" The words escaped before Jason could stop them. Fuck, he sounded like a whiny five-year-old instead of a rock god.

"Jason. You're my brother, and I know you. You've always had a thing for her."

A thing. She made it sound like something small and squeaky that hid under the bed at the first sign of danger. He didn't have a thing for her. It was full-blown love and had been since primary school. Since the first day Jo invited her to sit with them at choir practice. He'd lost his soul in the depths of her dark eyes that day. She'd never fucking noticed, though. Even when Chaya hit it big, she hadn't treated him like a rock god. He was just Jason, who forgot the words and drank too much and was never on time to rehearsals. Who ignored a rock god? Who fucking dared?

"I'm not going. No fucking way." If he had to watch Angel walk down the aisle to marry another man, he'd cry. He'd be on the front of every damn newspaper in the world with the headline JAY FELIX IS A PUSSY, because the woman he'd always loved threw him away for a muscle-bound psycho.

"You have to, Jay. Even if it breaks your heart to do it, she wants you there. What will the reporters say if you don't show up?"

"There won't be any. She doesn't give interviews and doesn't let any of them into her life." Jason tried to make it sound certain, but he wasn't. People took photos at weddings and all it took was one leaked to the press. Weddings were easy to crash — he'd even done it once or twice.

"You know there will be. A Chaya wedding means all of us. Grow a pair, put on a tie, and be there to support her. God knows how much she's done for you over the years."

Jason tried not to think about it. Every mess he'd gotten into, she'd seen it. Or most of them, at least. Those accusing eyes as she shook her head, disappointed again. Every time he got drunk, or the rare occasions he'd tried something stronger – fuck, trust a med student to know exactly what every illegal drug did to his body, plus describe what happened when people overdosed. She'd treated enough cases when she did her emergency department rotations. She had a rock god terrified to take drugs because nothing ruined his high like a fear of certain death. And the loss of his recording contract – she'd threatened that, too, if he couldn't pass a drug test.

"I'm busy. I can't go because I already have plans."

Jo snorted. "Bullshit. You don't have any plans for the rest of this week, let alone the rest of the year. You'll have to find a better excuse than that."

He stared at the invitation. The wedding was a whole year away at some beach resort in the south west. Wasn't that where her body had been dumped? When she'd been kidnapped and nearly died. No wonder the invitation resembled a funeral notice. Dark like her stage name: Angel Black.

Another name caught his eye. Well, not really a name. It was the absence of a name beside his.

She requested the company of Jason Felix *and partner*. Now that was a low blow, when she knew damn well she was the only life partner he'd ever dreamed about. Oh, sure there'd been other girls he'd considered, but only briefly. He shoved Audra out of his mind. Angel. Always, it came back to her.

"So I'll tell her you'll be there?" Jo ventured. "C'mon, Jason. It's time to grow up and face facts. She's just not that into you. You'd both be better off with other people."

No. Not before hell froze over and pigs flew and he put a gun to his head. Except he didn't want to die. Maybe she did. Maybe she'd taken the whole gothic costume to heart and now she wanted to die young. The ultimate tragedy.

Maybe it was time to face facts. If she married that psycho, he'd kill her for sure. But Jason didn't intend to settle for sloppy seconds if she survived. No, that ship had sailed. If Angel wanted to make her own bad decision, fuck her. Or not. He could get any girl he wanted and he'd prove it, too. By the time he turned up at her wedding, he'd be deliriously happy with his own partner, who he'd introduce to the ball-breaking bride on her wedding day.

"Sure. I'll be there. With a partner, too."

Silence. Jo sucked in a breath. "Jason, if you bring some fangirl to the wedding who blows you under the table, like you did at Sheila's wedding, she won't laugh it off. She's got family coming over from the Middle East for the wedding. If you embarrass her like that…shit, Jason, you're asking to get killed."

No, he didn't want some fangirl this time. She'd see through that as the passing fancy it was. "Don't be stupid. If she wants me at her wedding with my partner, then that's what she'll get. Not some fangirl. I'll be bringing my wife."

"Jason, tell me you haven't done anything stupid."

He grinned. "Stupid is for rock stars. I'm a hotel

manager now, or something like that. All respectable and shit. I should cut my hair and wear a shirt, maybe. But the hotel maids like it when I don't, so only occasionally."

"Oh, Jason, you didn't marry one of the hotel staff. Not that poor hotel maid. Please – "

The mention of Audra twisted the knife in his heart even deeper. Fuck her. Fuck them all. "Not a maid. No fucking way. I'm going to find a girl, make her madly in love with me, and we'll get married. All happily ever after and shit. Like a movie. Or the book I was reading last night."

"What book?"

A romance book Jason didn't feel like discussing with anyone right now. She'd say he was stupid. He pressed his lips together.

"Jason, no one marries a stranger and expects to be happy. That sort of thing only happens in fairy tales and romance novels. Not to real people. No one believes in happy endings any more."

"You'll see. My wife and me, we'll be so fucking happy, we'll stick the wedding couple in the shade. Tell her that, Jo." He ended the call and let out a breath he hadn't known he was holding.

A wife. One who wasn't a fangirl. He'd need a foreigner who had no idea who he was. One who didn't know his name, but who believed in fairy tales. Where the fuck was he going to find one of those?

EIGHT

"Are you an Australian citizen?"

This interview question was the kicker, Xan knew. No matter how qualified she was, wording this wrong could cost her a dream job. She couldn't wait to see the resort. Not for the first time, she wished the interviews had been conducted on the island, instead of at one of the hotels in town. "No. I'm on a working holiday visa that expires at the end of the year. I've travelled around Australia, working the peak season at several resorts on the east coast before taking the train across the country to Western Australia, where my journey brought me here to Broome. I was lucky enough to find a position that kept me here during the low season and I want to extend my stay for as long as possible. It's the sort of place you see in pictures and can't believe is real until you see the colours for yourself. Now, I don't want to leave."

"So you would consider extending your visa in order to stay here?" Max Meier asked, his voice so calm he sounded bored. From the way his whitened knuckles clutched the pen, Xan speculated that the answer to this meant far more to him that he was willing to admit.

"I would consider it, yes," Xan replied.

Triumph flashed in his eyes before it vanished. Xan hid her smile. The job was hers. She knew it.

"Romance Island Resort has an international clientele. I believe you mentioned experience in languages other than English?" Boredom had returned.

"After managing Broome Backpackers for the last five months, I believe I understand common phrases from more than fifty languages." When Meier's eyes widened in admiration, she delivered her punchline: "Especially 'Bloody hell, there's a frog in my bathroom!' though the swearing varies in intensity depending on the time of day and the state of undress of the guest."

Meier laughed. "So you're fluent in…?"

"English, Greek, Latin and French." Not that she expected to use the Greek or Latin her father had taught her, but it sounded good. Best not to mention it was ancient and not modern Greek, too.

"We get a lot of guests from Asia, so it's important that — "

"Qīngwā, katak, dādura. My pronunciation isn't perfect, I know, but that's frog in Chinese, Indonesian and Malay, and Hindi, I think. It's best that I don't share the swearing." Xan smiled sweetly. "I learn fast."

The interview wound down with a smattering of small talk and what Xan thought was a heart-felt handshake, at least on Meier's part. Was it her imagination or did he seem particularly desperate to fill this position?

She strode out of the Mangrove Hotel meeting room feeling more than a little smug. With the interview over, the afternoon spread out before her like a warm towel at the beach.

Except…all suited up as she was in this heat, a dip in the warm water of Roebuck Bay didn't appeal as much as it should. Better would be an ice-cold beer from the brewery. Xan turned her back on Town Beach and the hotel, where the next nervous-looking candidate had just met Max Meier.

A cold pint, a late lunch and a relaxing afternoon was what she deserved.

Kathy recognised her the moment she walked through the door, despite the suit, and Xan returned her friendly nod as she seated herself at a tiny table directly below one of the whirring fans.

Xan didn't need to do more than glance at the menu before Kathy stood at her side, order pad at the ready. "Same as usual?"

"Of course." Xan scanned the menu. "And the con carne. I haven't had lunch yet."

"Popular choice today. I'll see if we have any left."

Kathy returned with Xan's usual pint of ginger beer — alcoholic, of course; none of that kids' stuff. She confirmed that the kitchen could fill her lunch order before bustling up to deal with a group of wide-eyed tourists who stared avidly around as if they'd never seen old pearling memorabilia before. Perhaps they hadn't — after all, if the backpackers was busy, the other hotels in town had to be, too. So many new arrivals…

Xan had stared at the old black and white photos on the walls, too, on her first time here. The old sign from when the brewery had been a general store still hung over the bar, though the store had stopped trading decades ago, or that's what the tour guides said. She'd been the only one staring at the walls that day – everyone else had been transfixed by some celebrity who'd turned up and decided to treat his adoring fans. Some famous musician or other. She'd caught a glimpse of him. She wasn't sure what had irritated her the most: his arrogance or the sleazy way he'd surveyed his new-found harem. When she'd left that day, his party was well under way. She wondered which of the girls had been with him for more than a free meal. He'd evidently expected repayment for his largesse – God, men like that were everywhere. Luckily, she hadn't seen him again. Broome was better off without him.

Xan laughed quietly to herself. She'd only lived in the town for a few months and she was already as protective of it as a local. That's what this new job was all about, though – another reason for her to want to stay. She'd get to see even more of the surrounding countryside and ocean if she got the job at Romance Island Resort as she guided VIPs around. Helicopters and yachts and diving every day…she wouldn't want to give it up. Ah, that's what Jerome was for – to tempt her home when her working holiday got too good.

NINE

"What are you trying to do, kill me?" Norman's whining voice set her teeth on edge.

Don't tempt me, Phuong thought, setting down the cooking oil. She glanced at the cutting board, where a suitable blade sat between the chopped meat and vegetables she planned to stir fry for dinner.

"First all this weird Asian food with rice and now peanut oil? Don't you know I'm allergic to peanuts? If I didn't know better, I'd say you don't want to be my wife. Where are the potatoes? Steak? Real food that normal people have? Didn't your mum teach you to cook properly back home in Bangkok, Fiona?"

In Singapore, they'd had a cook, just like in the residential college dorm she'd lived in until she'd moved in with Norman a month ago. But she bit her tongue instead of correcting him. She'd grown resigned to letting him anglicise her name to Fiona instead of mangling her real one.

Phuong arranged her expression in what she hoped was an apologetic smile. "No, sorry."

His fist slammed into the counter, making her jump. "Then fucking learn! You want to earn your keep and stay here, learn to cook real food!"

Inwardly seething, Phuong lowered her eyes as she nodded. This was what she got, looking for a husband on a mail-order bride website. The sort who couldn't get a girl any other way. She'd leave him the moment she got her citizenship, she promised herself. In the meantime, she just had to put up with him.

"So what's for dinner tonight?" he demanded. A nasty glint in his eye warned her that this wasn't over.

"Pork stir fry with – "

"No more fucking Asian rabbit food! I want steak or a roast!"

Phuong moved to the freezer, her knuckles turning white as she gripped the door and peered inside. "We don't have any. I'll have to do some shopping and we can have steak tomorrow."

"With fucking potatoes. And mushy peas." He scrunched his eyebrows fiercely so they met over his nose. "You'll order the shopping online tonight to be delivered tomorrow when I get home."

Phuong forced out another smile and a nod.

"I'll order pizza tonight, but I won't be so lenient next time. When I get off the phone, I expect you in the bedroom. Ready for me."

With numb fingers, Phuong untied her apron and

headed for the dreaded bedroom.

Hours later, when Norman's beer-fuelled snoring told her that the ordeal was over for the night, Phuong pressed her thighs together to still the aching between them from Norman's rough lovemaking. There was no love in it, or even desire on her part. He disgusted her, but she didn't dare say so. She got free rent and board, and this was his price.

She threw the bedclothes off and padded to the apartment's tiny living area. Her laptop still sat on the table from submitting the grocery order, so she flicked it on again and watched the screen glow to life. Like she had almost every evening since moving in with Norman, Phuong logged on to the mail-order bride website where she'd first corresponded with him. He'd been the first to respond to her ad and she'd seized the opportunity to live with a man who promised to take care of her so she'd never need to work a day in her life.

She hadn't expected to be locked in his apartment, cooking and cleaning, until he returned from work to use her body as if she were a prostitute. If only she'd known that he spent most of his annual vacation time in places like Bangkok, banging prostitutes who didn't require him to be anything more than a paying customer. No wonder he didn't know how to treat a woman. The only excitement she felt in the bedroom was when he was done or if he started snoring, so she could retreat to the shower and scrub the feel of his touch off her skin.

Men with six-packs who treated women like princesses didn't need to find a bride on the internet. She'd known that, but every day with Norman was more of a struggle.

Not for the first time, she considered doing what her school friend's sister had to pay her way through university — Lin had paid for her board and nursing degree by performing cash-in-hand prostitution work for patients and staff in the hospitals where she did her practical placements. No, she couldn't. Letting one man use her body was bad enough. Taking all comers…she'd scrub her skin raw after every one.

Resolutely, she opened the message page for the dating site where she'd kept every one of Norman's messages of love and devotion. Lies, she knew now, but so were all fairy tales. This was the quickest way to achieve her end: to become an Australian citizen, then get an interest-free government loan for the final year of her degree at a third the price she'd pay as a Singaporean citizen.

Today, Norman's saccharin-sweet words didn't soothe her the way they used to. Perhaps because she recognised their falseness.

Idly, she clicked on one of the unread messages from some other man whose profile was a sculpted, headless torso, like something cropped from the cover of a romance novel. Not that she could read those much with Norman around — she kept the extensive library of ebooks on her phone a carefully hidden secret. Norman might explode with rage if he knew other men were better at sex than he was, or that women actually enjoyed it. He made cavemen look enlightened.

Mr Six-Pack's message was short:

"I'm looking for a woman who knows all fairy tales are lies, but who still hopes one might come true."

Reflexively, Phuong clicked on his profile. Mr Six-Pack

was a gym junkie, he admitted, who went by the name of Lucky Jason. He worked on a remote island, but it was lonely and he wanted to share his living accommodation with someone who could brighten the darkness at night. Or so he said. She laughed softly before clapping a hand over her mouth at the thought that she might wake Norman. His snores continued, like he was sawing down a tree with his nose in his sleep, so she breathed a sigh of relief and returned to ogling Jason's abs. Desire flooded her for the first time in months. If only she'd received his message before Norman's, maybe she'd be stroking those muscles in bed right now...

She hit the reply button. "Which fairy tale did you have in mind, and which character are you? The big bad wolf, the woodcutter or Prince Charming?" Before she could think better of it, she sent the message.

The response came back almost instantly: "What would you like me to be? I can cut down everyone keeping you from me, carry you off to my castle like Prince Charming, then turn into the big bad wolf and eat you all up until you scream for joy."

"That only happens in books," she whispered to herself, then typed the words and fired them off.

Lucky Jason had an answer for that, too: "One day, some romance author will write books about us and a million lonely women will crave the sort of sex you only have to ask for."

Arrogant much? "No one's that good. What if I'm after Prince Charming, a man who loves me, listens to me and wants to take care of me, and I'm not interested in sex?"

"Prince Charming is a prick who'll smother you and turn

jealous if you look at anyone else. He'll lock you in a tower and never let you out. And he wouldn't know what to do with his own cock, let alone your body. Prince where-do-I-put-my-prick. That's not me, babe."

But it was Norman.

"No? You don't get jealous? What do you do when your girl looks at another man?"

"Grin and wink at the guy while my arm's around her. He'll never be me and never have what I do, but that's cool. Not everyone's as awesome as me. Let me show you, babe."

She gasped at his audacity, the sheer arrogance of the man…but even the typed words made her more aroused than Norman ever had. Aroused at a man who used a stock photo for a profile picture. "Show me what you really look like first."

"What do you mean? The site's rules say no face, cock or arse pictures, so I stuck my six-pack on there. You don't like muscles, babe?"

"They don't look real. Show me what you really look like." She slowly exhaled, knowing she'd effectively ended the conversation. Lucky Jason's six-pack was as fictional as his sexual prowess. Big bad wolf eating her, indeed.

She left the laptop and headed to the kitchen to dry the dishes. Lucky Jason wasn't so lucky tonight, but then neither was she.

Phuong returned to the laptop when she'd put away the last beer glass. To her surprise, a blurry picture of a man's muscled tummy beside the edge of a keyboard sat on the screen. "Satisfied?" said the message above it.

"No," she replied. "You could've pulled that photo off the internet, too. Give me proof of life. Take a picture with today's newspaper."

"We don't get newspapers out here. I live on a deserted island. Tell me your real name and I'll write it across my abs for you."

If he mangled her name or called her Fiona like Norman, she'd delete every damn message and never speak to him again. "It's Phuong."

Seconds ticked by without a response. Phuong glanced at the clock on the oven. If she didn't go to bed soon, she wouldn't get enough sleep before Norman insisted she make breakfast for him.

She glanced back and was greeted by another blurry picture, but this one had the letters P-H-U wavering across his skin. She held her breath as another picture appeared, this time bearing a wonky O, a back-to-front N and a tailed G that ended by guiding her eye to the treasure trail vanishing into the waistband of his shorts. Then a final shot with all six letters.

Before she could type a response, he added a line of text: "How do you pronounce it?"

"Rhymes with thong, only with an F." Wonders never ceased. A second point to Lucky Jason – one for actually having a six-pack, and one for caring about getting her name right.

"I want to see you wearing one so I can take it off with my teeth."

That made him an American, Phuong guessed, sighing. Lucky Jason was too good to be true. He couldn't give her Aussie citizenship, so she'd be stuck with Norman.

"Just don't bite my feet. I'm looking for an Australian man who knows thongs come in pairs and who'll wear them with me as we go for a walk on the beach. Is there one of those on your deserted island? Don't think so."

She switched her computer off and put it away, wishing for just a moment she'd waited for someone like Jason instead of settling for neurotic Norman. Squeezing into the apartment's only bed beside Norman, she dreamed of something better. Someone better. Hoping that one day, she'd be free to choose.

TEN

Her day had to get better. It had to. Oh, in God's name, what was that racket?

The long, loud note of someone pressing the shit out of their horn made Xan stick her head out of the office. A guest had almost reversed his hire car into the drinks truck. Instead of attempting to manoeuvre around the truck, or waiting for the driver to finish his delivery, the idiot punched his car horn again and started swearing at the driver to move.

Xan scanned the parking lot, but the foul-mouthed guest was the only person there.

She found the truck driver in the kitchen, lifting boxes onto the counter for Adele. Every time his biceps flexed, Adele cooed over them.

"What's happening out there?" the delivery guy asked.

"Someone nearly crashed into your truck and for some

reason this upset him, so he's blaming you for it." Xan shrugged. "Let him wait. The only cars that can't get out of that parking lot are the staff ones you're parked in front of, and we won't need them until Adele finishes work in an hour."

Adele flashed a grateful smile.

"Only an hour to go? Same as me," the driver drawled, eyeing Adele.

Xan returned to the office and month-end reports. This would go so much faster if Emily hadn't messed up the data entry on all the invoices. Tomorrow, she'd have to sit the girl down and explain it again. But right now, the fastest way to fix this was to redo it all herself. One invoice at a time.

If only she'd gotten that resort job. It'd been three weeks since her interview and she hadn't heard anything, though they'd said she'd know within a week. That meant a rejection letter, she was sure of it. They'd probably found some Aussie who'd grown up bilingual, speaking Chinese or whatever they needed their tour guide to talk in. If she'd known she'd need Chinese, she'd have dropped French and picked up the new language in a heartbeat, way back in high school. Even the memory of her French teacher's expression as Xan mauled the woman's native tongue was enough to make her wish she'd had another option.

Invoices. Xan forced herself to think of invoices and not what might have been. Her bad luck now would surely lead to an awesome opportunity soon enough. Something always came up.

Six corrections later, her phone buzzed. Xan didn't recognise the number, aside from knowing it was a Broome landline, so she answered cautiously, "Hi, this is Xan."

"Ms Lane? It's Max Meier, the manager here at the Romance Island Resort. Sorry it's taken so much time to get back to you, but it's taken this long to clarify matters with the Department of Immigration. They can't extend a visa like yours, but they can transition it into a skilled migrant visa with a view to…" He continued, but Xan only half listened to jargon, numbers and a boring story about bureaucracy.

What did it matter? He'd evidently given the job to someone else. If this was his rambling way of justifying it, she'd have preferred the stock-standard rejection letter in the post, thank you. It was far more satisfying to shred the letter into little pieces than to listen politely to someone deliver the same message until she could bite out a false but cheerful farewell.

A string of words caught her attention. "Wait – what?"

"I said we can only offer you the job if you're willing to commit to at least a full year, with the possibility of extending your contract over the next three years after that." Meier sucked in a breath. "But if you cease working with us, you'll have two weeks to leave the country and the resort will pay for your flights."

He wasn't rejecting her? But a year…or even four of them…she'd have to talk to her parents. Not to mention Jerome. If she lived here that long, maybe she'd never want to leave.

Of course, the resort job could suck donkey's balls and maybe she'd want to leave after a week. Unlikely, but possible. If that happened, she'd be back on a plane to the UK earlier than she'd intended. But the resort would pay for it…

"Ms Lane?"

"Sorry." The possibilities kept multiplying before her eyes. "I'm at work at the moment, so I can't really discuss this here. Can you send those contracts through so I can take a look at them? I should be able to give you an answer tomorrow."

"There's the visa documents, too. Quite a lot of paperwork. We'd need all of it filled in as soon as possible, as the visa application takes some time and you can't start work until it's approved."

Which bit of 'I'm at work and can't discuss this' did he not understand? Xan wasn't sure she wanted to work for a demanding boss who ignored any kind of professional ethics. Plus, if she didn't get along with him, the moment she quit, she'd be shipped back to the UK on the next plane – end of adventure.

Movement caught her eye and Xan couldn't help staring as a man wearing nothing but a towel that barely met around his hips strode across the courtyard toward her. She had to get off the phone now. Drooling was imminent.

"I understand. I'll get back to you tomorrow." Before Meier could say anything else, she ended the call.

"Yes? Can I help you?" Xan addressed the six-pack rapidly approaching before lifting her gaze over his defined chest to his thunderous expression.

"I found this in the shower," he grumbled, opening one fist.

Xan caught a glimpse of green before the frog made a flying leap for freedom. Taut-and-Towelled launched himself into the air after the miscreant, throwing both arms up to catch it. The towel flew apart like the wings of an angel, displaying everything he had to offer his future bride. Xan didn't need a camera to remember this – the image of his flying wedding tackle was burned into her retinas. The rest of him wasn't half-bad, either. And he caught frogs naked – quite an achievement, though one he didn't seem particularly proud of.

Flying Frog Man dove for his towel and wrapped it around his hips once more, mumbling something as he hurried back to the bathroom.

And that was why Xan had chosen to work in a backpackers hostel. Every day had new surprises in store. Even she hadn't guessed that today would include the best flying tackle she'd ever seen and a job offer. What else would the day hold?

Her chiming computer brought her thoughts back to the present. Sighing, Xan returned to the monthly accounts. The sooner she was finished, the sooner she could open the email from Meier that had just popped up in her inbox.

Xan wasn't sure whether to buy celebratory champagne or bugger-the-whole-bloody-world bourbon on her way home. Maybe both. She'd decide what to drink once she'd read Meier's email. It's not like alcohol went to waste at her place. Today might not be a bourbon day, but tomorrow might deserve a double.

ELEVEN

If she'd been a bourbon drinker, Phuong would have downed a whole bottle happily. As it was, they only had beer and it wasn't exactly a breakfast food.

Phuong had managed to stay away from her messages for thirty-five hours, until Norman had insisted on pancakes for breakfast.

"You're useless in the kitchen. These are nothing like my mum used to make. These aren't fit for dogs!" Norman shook the offending pancake in her face before dropping it in the bin. It didn't matter that every other identical pancake she'd made had been eaten with grunts of what she'd assumed were approval. Today, they weren't good enough. "You better not mess up dinner, or I'll throw you out of the house and find someone better!"

He closed the door behind him and ground the key in the deadlock, effectively imprisoning her in the third-floor apartment.

Tears sprang to her eyes at the thought that she'd endured a month of this torture without a thing to show for it. Still she was no closer to getting her citizenship or finishing her degree. Phuong grabbed her laptop and gripped the keyboard as she waited for it to power up. This time, she didn't even glance at Norman's messages — her eyes darted to the new message waiting from Lucky Jason. Whispering a prayer, she clicked on it.

She gasped at the gallery of photos Jason had sent her. A weird angled shot, showing his abs and his shorts in the blurred foreground as the picture focussed on his thong-clad feet on the sand. In the second picture, he held out a pair of pink ladies' thongs with a long, sandy beach in the background. Phuong scrolled down, only to discover he'd taken the shoes to half a dozen picturesque spots and photographed each one. A jetty, a tiny beach beneath rust-coloured cliffs, palm trees caressing white sand, his feet knee deep in water, with what looked like baby sharks swimming around his legs, with a final shot of the sunset framed between the same pair of women's footwear.

He'd only written one line to go with them: "I'm looking for a woman who can fill these shoes."

She laughed at the Cinderella reference, knowing that no self-respecting fairy godmother would grant a girl rubber-soled thongs. Jason and his talk of fairy tales.

"Where on Earth do you live?" Phuong fired back, wiping her tears away. Jason lived in paradise. He'd surely have his pick of beautiful women there.

But there was no response. He wasn't online, or he wasn't listening.

Phuong decided to work off her frustration by doing the things she hated most. She scrubbed the bathroom, cleaned the toilet, mopped all the tiles and vacuumed every bit of the floor, checking her laptop as she passed, hoping for an answer that never came.

She vacuumed mummified fly corpses out of the sliding door tracks and window frames, emptied the kitchen cabinets, wiped them down and replaced everything.

Jason had vanished off the face of the Earth, if he even existed.

Phuong loaded a piece of pork into the roasting pan, obeying the instructions on the packaging as she set the temperature and timer. Whatever she did to the meat, it wouldn't satisfy Norman, but he'd at least be mercifully silent for the few minutes he had his mouth full.

Grabbing a handful of sugar snap peas from the fridge, she sat in front of her laptop as she crunched through her snack. As if he'd sensed her presence, a new message from Jason popped up on the screen.

Eight words: "Romance Island Resort. The loneliest island on Earth."

A resort? Phuong snorted. He'd have women hanging off him at every turn. If there was such a place. A quick search revealed that the island did exist and some of the pictures on the resort's website resembled those Jason had sent her.

"What's wrong with you that you can't get a date on Romance Island?" she typed. There. Now it'd come out. Maybe his face was horribly disfigured and no one could look at him. Maybe he'd suffered a horrific accident so he couldn't see, hear or speak.

"I can get a date or a one night stand or a holiday romance from almost any woman who sets foot on the island. They can't resist me. But love, commitment? No one wants that any more. They just want what I can do for them and they're gone, taking a piece of my heart with them."

"That's not true," she began, then hesitated. She wasn't looking for love or long-term commitment – just what an Australian man could give her to further her career. Was she so different? It's not like she'd looked for love from Norman. She wanted to be free of him as soon as possible. Erasing her first line, she replaced it with: "You must have known some really horrible, mercenary women."

As if by magic, she'd unleashed the floodgates. Jason's responses flowed thick and fast, relating years of pain at casual relationships that never lasted. Women who weren't enough for him, who wanted to drain him dry and leave him a lifeless husk.

Like Norman was doing to her.

The scrape of booted feet on the doormat sent Phuong into a panic – she'd lost track of the time and Norman was home already. She hadn't even prepared the vegetables. Slamming her laptop shut, she stowed it in the bag and hurried to the kitchen. Norman could never know she'd been talking to another man – he'd go ballistic and try to take her laptop away from her.

She couldn't allow that to happen. Jason was the only thing keeping her sane. And maybe, just maybe, she could help him, too.

TWELVE

Xan skimmed through the documents as she ate her dinner alone at home that evening. The Chinese takeaway did the best roast pork and she'd decided to treat herself tonight.

The more she read, the more she became convinced that she'd been offered her dream job. Nevertheless, she couldn't accept it without speaking to her family and, more importantly, Jerome. He hadn't replied to her emails in a while, and she'd been so busy with work that she'd been too tired to call him most nights. But this was important – she'd track him down by dawn, if it killed her.

Who to call first? Her parents would be easy – they supported her in everything she did – but she didn't want to tell them about the new job if Jerome didn't want her to take it. Better that they never knew about it at all.

She tried Jerome, but got no answer, so she left him a short voicemail asking him to call her as soon as he received her message, or tell her when to call back.

Fine. Her parents it would be, then.

"Finally!" Mum huffed before even bothering with a 'hello'. "I thought you'd forgotten all about us. Having so much fun in Australia that you forgot about the people who love and care for you here at home?"

Despite herself, Xan laughed. "Yeah, Mum. Doing the monthly accounts for a backpacker hostel in between rescuing the tourists from the resident wildlife is so thrilling, I've started applying for other jobs to save myself."

"Wildlife? What kind of wildlife?" Her mother turned pale. "Tell me you're not catching snakes and other dangerous things, turning into something like that crazy crocodile man. He died, you know."

"No, Mum, I haven't caught a single crocodile, though I heard one might have moved into the mangroves near Streeter's Jetty in town. I heard it from one of the tour guides who saw the tracks. More likely kids with dirt bikes, but you never know. I'm sure I've told you about the frogs in the bathrooms at the backpackers." Xan didn't have to force a smile. Flying Frog Man was her favourite guest this week, hands down.

"What kind of hotel has frogs in the bathroom? It sounds like a dive, Xanthe, honey. With all your qualifications and things, surely you can get a better job in a place without vermin."

Mum gave her the best openings. "Actually, I received a job offer this morning. A luxury resort on its own island just north of here wants me to work for them, organising activities for their celebrity guests and stuff. It looks really good, but they want me to stay longer than I'd planned.

Definitely past Christmas. Maybe even longer than that."

"Really?" Mum peered at the screen, as if trying to search Xan's expression through the thousands of miles separating them. "Are you sure that's what you want? We love you and we'd love to have you home for Christmas, of course, but it seems like you've already given up so much for your trip. A good job at the school where your father teaches, your lovely flat, and that boyfriend of yours. Is living in Australia really worth giving up all of that?"

The flat hadn't been lovely at all – it had been tiny, with walls so thin you heard what the neighbours were watching on TV or, worse, what noises they made in bed. Teaching English was hardly her dream job and Jerome…she hadn't given him up at all. They were engaged and the wedding would happen when she got back.

"…but I suppose that wasn't as hard as I expected…"

Xan shook herself out of her meandering thoughts as she realised her mother was still rambling.

"Is he the reason you've moved to Australia?" Mum finished plaintively.

"Is who? And I haven't moved to Australia. I'm just here on a working holiday, a bit of a break after finishing university before – "

"That half-wit ex-boyfriend of yours! He should have fought harder to make you stay, but it's his loss."

Had her mother been drinking? Surely she remembered the fancy family dinner where Xan and Jerome had announced their engagement. Xan hadn't taken the ring off since. "Mum – "

"You deserve better. Maybe you can find some rugged Australian man while you're over there. That's why you broke it off with that boy here, didn't you? You knew what he was like and didn't want a bar of it. I always knew he was bad news…"

"MUM! What are you talking about? Since when is Jerome bad news?" Xan wanted to reach through the screen and shake her mother. None of this made sense.

"Since he got little Kelly from up the road pregnant. He's going to marry her, too, when she'd old enough, so now she's proudly walking up and down the street in all weather, just so everyone can see her ring, resting on that swelling belly of hers."

Kelly? Xan racked her brain for anyone they knew by that name. There was that kid up the road she used to babysit on occasion, but she was only a teenager – barely into high school. "Which Kelly, Mum? The one I'm thinking of is only fourteen. Jerome knew her because he babysat with me a few times, or picked me up from there when it was too late to walk, but he couldn't…" He couldn't have a baby with some kid when he was meant to marry me, was what Xan wanted to say, but the words stuck in her throat.

"She's sixteen now. You've been away for a while, Xanthe. After you broke up with him, that boy must have moved on right away. He always did want a wife and kids. Guess he got both in one hit. You did good when you broke up with him. I always knew there was something off about him…"

Xan lost track of her mother's words again, but this time she didn't care. Twenty-six-year-old Jerome having a baby with Kelly, who was still a kid in school herself? He couldn't…he couldn't…the diamond ring on her finger blurred in the onslaught of tears. Tears she couldn't shed in front of her mother.

Blinking furiously, Xan made excuses and ended the call. What in hell had just happened?

It was a lie, she decided. Her mother's idea of an April Fool's joke, though it wasn't April yet. She'd check Jerome's social media profile and try calling him again.

She scrolled through her list of contacts, looking for his name, but couldn't find it. Swearing, she entered his name in the search box and waited for his profile to come up. There he was – she clicked on it and her slow connection flashed an error message. Uttering a few more swear-words, Xan refreshed the page and dialled his number on her phone.

The phone trilled in her ear as the page loaded. Most of the content wasn't showing because she had to be on his friends list to see it, the page told her. What in hell did that mean? Of course they were friends. They were getting fucking married. Unless he'd broken ties with her so sneakily she hadn't even noticed…

Jerome's profile picture popped up on the screen. There, for all the world to see, were Jerome and Kelly, kissing.

"Hullo?" Jerome's sleepy voice answered.

Xan's blood boiled. "You're a fucking wanker. And a paedophile. But mostly a wanker. I hope she kills you in your sleep when she wakes up and realises what you've done to her, you sick wanker!" She hung up.

Jerome could go screw himself before she'd ever speak to him again, let alone look at him. To hell with marriage and family and settling down.

Where were those contracts? Feverishly, Xan started

filling out forms as fast as her fingers would go. Her Australian adventure just got kicked up a notch. She was going to give that resort's celebrity guests such a good time, they'd never want to leave. Just like her.

Before she opened the bourbon, Xan had one more call to make.

Meier answered on the second ring.

"Hi, it's Xan Lane. I've read the documents you sent me and I only have one question. There's a clause in the contract that says in the first six months, either you or I can terminate my employment with a day's notice for no reason at all. With my work visa, that basically means if you take a dislike to anything I do, I have zero job security and I can be deported on a moment's notice. Can that clause be removed?"

"Is that your only question, Ms Lane?" It sounded like he held his breath.

Shouldn't it be? Xan's instincts tingled, but she couldn't think of anything else she wanted to question in the contract. This was a test, surely. "Yes. If that clause is gone, and my employment is dependent on my conduct and all the normal employment criteria a permanent employee is entitled to, I'll sign it."

"Then we have a deal, Ms Lane. I'll amend the contract and have a fresh copy for you to sign when you arrive at the resort. I'll arrange for you to be flown over on the Friday before you start, so you can spend a weekend here in paradise as a guest before starting your job on the Monday morning. Now, shall we discuss your start date?"

Yes. Xan let out a breath she hadn't known she was holding and smiled. Jerome could go to hell for all she cared. She'd earned a stint in paradise and they didn't allow snakes like him through the gate.

THIRTEEN

Only half listening to Norman's gloating tale of how he'd managed to charge some woman twice what the job was worth without her noticing, Phuong reached for the olive oil, but her fingers wrapped around the neck of the peanut oil bottle. Luckily, she realised her mistake, so she quickly corrected it before Norman could see. She emptied the olive oil bottle over the potatoes and shook it to get the last drops out before adding the pan to the oven. She lowered the empty oil bottle carefully into the recycling bin so the clink didn't interrupt Norman, then jotted cooking oil on the shopping list. Good thing he insisted steak had to be fried in butter, or she'd be in trouble.

She watched the butter melt and added a fat t-bone to the pan, setting the heat to low so it would cook all the way through like Norman liked it. Or he said he liked it. Yesterday he'd insisted he wanted his steak well-done. Who knew what he liked today?

A clammy hand crept beneath her skirt and clamped around her bum-cheek, squeezing almost to the point of pain. She'd welcome a cuddle from a snake instead of a grope from Norman, and she hated snakes. Damp lips pressed to the back of her neck. Phuong suppressed a shudder as he whispered, "We should have sex to celebrate."

No, we damn well shouldn't, Phuong thought, but she resigned herself to it anyway. She reached to turn off the steak, but Norman grabbed her hand.

"I'll be hungry after this. Don't keep me waiting for my dinner." Not letting go of her hand, he led her to the bedroom.

Ten nauseating minutes later, she dashed back to the kitchen as Norman dealt with the used condom and washed up.

Too late. The steak was burned around the edges. Phuong flipped it and reached for a knife to cut away the blackened bits, but Norman had already left the bathroom and he was watching her every move. Sighing, she dropped the knife back in the drawer. Good thing she hadn't cooked any steak for herself – she'd have trouble eating anything tonight.

Maybe if she hid the burned bits under a thick layer of gravy, Norman might not notice she'd singed his steak. He wasn't exactly the most observant man. If he had been, he might have noticed her distraction over the last few weeks, as she'd spent all of her waking moments responding to Jason's messages or dreaming about being in bed with him instead of two-minute Norman. She'd given Jason her email

address, so she no longer needed her laptop to talk to him —
now she could access his messages on her phone. And the
last one had been his most persuasive yet — he'd asked her
to come to him, so he could propose to her properly and be
her…what had he called it? Knight in shining armour? But
only after she kissed him, turning him from a frog into a
prince again. Him and his fairy tales, so far removed from
real life it made her existence even more depressing.

Whisking gravy mix and hot water in a pan, Phuong
carefully added more water from the kettle. If Norman
found a single lump, he'd whine about her uselessness for
half an hour. Though if he did, he might miss the burned
meat…and which was the lesser of two evils? Maybe if she
got him a beer, he'd be even less perceptive…

Phuong gave Norman a perfunctory smile as she set his
plate before him. Overcooked peas and potatoes swam in
the swamp of gravy that had oozed off his enormous steak.
While he surveyed her handiwork, she dashed to the
kitchen for his beer.

"Are you trying to poison me?" he grunted. "Where's
your dinner?"

She'd never thought of that, though she wished she had.
Phuong recovered quickly. "I wanted to serve you first."
She hoped her batted eyelashes distracted him enough.

She dished up a small plate of the potatoes for herself
and poured a thin veneer of gravy over the top. Sitting
down across from Norman, she cut a small piece of potato
and placed it in her mouth. She chewed with feigned delight
and forced herself to swallow the starchy vegetable even as
it choked her.

Norman seemed satisfied. He tucked into his own

dinner, dribbling gravy down his front with careless disregard for the work she'd have getting the stains out of his work shirt or the tablecloth. When he took his first bite of steak, he chewed a couple of times before his eyebrows knitted over his nose. Phuong's heart sank.

He spat the mouthful onto the tablecloth, leaving a splatter of gravy and spit that reached her plate. "You're the worst fucking cook in the world, Fiona. How many times do I have to tell you I like my steak medium? This one's fucking burned, look." He pointed at the blackened beef on the table.

If he hadn't insisted on fucking while she was supposed to be cooking, and told her that today he wanted it only half-cooked, then maybe she could have met his demands. Nothing she did would ever be good enough.

"I'm sorry," she said. What else could she say? She wondered if Jason would make her life a living hell like this. If any other man would.

"You should be. I give you a good fucking and you can't even make me dinner. You should go back to Thailand and working as a whore. You're not good for anything else." He gulped down a third of his beer.

I'm not from Thailand and there's nothing good about getting naked with you, she wanted to scream for the millionth time, but she stayed silent.

He emptied his beer and slammed the bottle on the table. "What are you good for?" he demanded, his voice dangerously low. "Tell me why I should let you stay and be my wife."

She knew what he wanted to hear. He wanted her to repeat the phone-sex lines he'd demanded in the endless messages on the website where they'd met. "I'm good in bed. I can go all night, any way you want to, but only for you, Norman."

He grinned. "Get me another beer."

She did.

He drank slowly, eyeing her over the lip of the bottle. "Tell me why I should fuck you and not some other Thai whore."

Phuong swallowed. Only the thought of not getting her citizenship forced the words out. "I'm better than any whore because I'm all yours. Every inch, every night, all night and no one else can have me but you. You make me so hot, Norman."

"Good girl," he slurred. The second empty beer landed on the table. "Get me another one and I'll give it to you all night, Fiona." He reached into his lap to fondle what Phuong knew was limp and little and lasted less time than any man should.

He made her wait until he'd finished six beers and all of the supposedly inedible steak before he beckoned her back to the bedroom. Only thoughts of Jason's sexy body got her through the next fifteen minutes, as Norman struggled to get it up and blamed it, as he did everything, on her.

When he finally withdrew and she thought her ordeal was over for the night, she heard him say, "Now I want a massage, whore, for making me work so hard."

"Oh, but we're out of massage oil," she lamented.

A stinging slap landed on her thigh. "Then use cooking oil, whore. Give me my fucking money's worth and massage me!"

Forcing her clenched hands to stay by her sides, Phuong

left the bed and headed to the kitchen. She grabbed the only bottle of oil in the cupboard and returned to Norman. This was the last time she'd ever touch him, she swore. When he started snoring, she'd pack her things and leave him forever. Slowly, she upended the oil bottle over his back and started to rub it into his skin.

FOURTEEN

The world seemed so alien below, all red rocks and grey-green scrub that clung to the rocks as desperately as she'd clutched the idea of her future with Jerome. But just like the storms that wreaked havoc up here, Cyclone Kelly had put paid to that dream and she could have the bastard. Ha. Her own bastard baby and his wanker of a father. Poor girl. She was too young to know what she was getting into…but she had to know she was stealing another woman's boyfriend. How many times had Kelly asked to see Xan's engagement ring so she could ooh and ah over it?

Xan rubbed her finger, which still felt bare after she'd torn off the ring and sold it at the pawnbroker. She gave the money to the women's shelter in town, knowing they needed the money more than she did. The coordinator had invited her in for tea, as a token of thanks for her gift, and Xan had been too polite to refuse. For fifteen minutes, she'd sat at the long dining table, reminiscent of school dining halls back in the UK, drinking her scalding tea until footsteps behind her told her she wasn't alone. When she turned, she met the eyes of a woman who looked as lost as Xan felt.

They'd stared at each other for what felt like forever, recognising the inner void that they both shared and yet didn't share. It was a lonely, echoing emptiness inside the impenetrable shell Xan had to maintain to make sure no one saw her loss. She'd loved and then had her heart ripped out and fed to a crocodile. Yet somehow she kept on living, shame settling on her like a shroud. Shame that she'd been foolish enough to trust her heart to a man who only wanted to use it for bait to catch something as heartless as him.

Xan hadn't stayed long after that. She wasn't as finished as these women seemed to feel – she had a new job and all her life ahead of her. Without that bastard Jerome to limit her, who knew how high she could fly? And in a helicopter, no less.

Yet now she was up here, she felt so small and insignificant. This huge country with its rugged, unconquered landscape was nothing like home. Not even like the relatively civilised Cable Beach near town. The Dampier Peninsula and the Buccaneer Archipelago beyond had only a few scattered structures on them, connected by tiny ribbons of road.

"Where's the island?" Xan asked dully, scanning the drowned hills that formed the Buccaneer Archipelago.

"It's coming up on the horizon in a few minutes. Your first time out there?" Shou glanced at her and Xan nodded. "Then I'll do a proper fly-by to orient you before we land.

Most staff take the carrier boat; the only times I've flown staff to and from the island are when there's an emergency."

Xan waited for him to continue, but as the silence stretched between them, she found she needed to break it. "And? What sort of emergencies?"

Shou seemed intent on the horizon. "The sort that you hope won't happen again at a resort like Romance Island. They've had far too many of them lately. That's all I can say. Look, this is a high-class resort, the sort that offers a high degree of privacy for its guests. We all keep its secrets or we don't work here any more. It's that simple. You may find out about past events if your job requires it, but it's very much a need-to-know basis where nobody really needs to know. You'll get used to it. Most of the people who come out here are those with secrets of their own – the staff and the guests. Some are running from something and the rest are hiding something. Which are you?"

Xan summoned a wan smile. "That's my secret, and you don't need to know."

"Touché." Shou extended his hand to point at a shadow on the horizon. "There's the resort. It doesn't look like much now, but wait until you see..."

The bump on the water resolved into colours – cream, green and a milky blue, arranged in two lines, no, wait, a v-shape. No, it was...

"Bloody hell. No wonder it's called Romance Island. That can't be natural." Xan stared at the heart-shaped island with a lagoon in the middle. Jetties on either side made it look like it had been pierced by a giant Cupid's arrow. Kind of like her heart still felt, but without the love such a missile was supposed to inspire.

"It mostly is. There are a couple of others the same shape up and down the coast, but this one's the biggest and the lagoon's actually a big rock pool, one of the few places calm enough for coral to grow. It's meant to have some of the best snorkelling and diving this side of Rowley Shoals." Shou peered wistfully at the water as the helicopter moved in a tight turn around the island.

"Meant to? You mean you haven't been in yourself?" Xan asked.

Shou shrugged. "The resort's tour guide promised she'd take me, but she left in a bit of a hurry before I could take her up on the offer."

"I'm a qualified dive master. I could take you," Xan offered.

The helicopter pilot stared at her in what looked like surprise. "Really? Well, if you get time, just let me know. I'd appreciate it."

For the first time in what felt like days, Xan laughed. "I always make time for diving. When the weather's right and with a dive site on my doorstep, I won't let anything stop me from taking a daily dip. The last time I dived was Ningaloo, though, before I came to Broome, so I can't wait to get back into it."

Another long look followed before Shou said abruptly, "Hang on. Coming in to land. Welcome to Romance Island Resort. I hope you enjoy your stay."

Xan settled back in her seat, mulling over the mysteries Shou had hinted at. First were the emergencies he wouldn't discuss. What had happened at the resort that had to be kept so quiet? Was it anything to do with her predecessor, who'd left so suddenly? And what was with the strange looks? Did Shou know something about the island that she didn't?

Then there was Meier's easy acceptance of her contract variation. That didn't sit right. She'd never had a job in Australia where they hadn't told her that the probation period was a standard condition they couldn't change, but then she'd never been on this new visa, either.

If she didn't know better, she'd swear there was something suspicious about this whole resort, but no one else in Broome had a bad word to say about the place. Unless you counted the cost of staying there, of course. Everyone wanted to visit and they bemoaned the fact that they couldn't afford it.

Well, for now, it was her home, and Xan was determined to unravel the mystery behind this place. She slid out of the helicopter and breathed deeply. Salt, heat and humidity, with the sibilance of waves breaking endlessly on a beach somewhere through the palm trees and pandanus. If she closed her eyes, she could be standing on Cable Beach.

Except there weren't any vehicles on the island — this place was an eco-resort, one that claimed to be so environmentally friendly even the wildlife welcomed guests to the island.

Maybe the island's secrets involved the wildlife. Xan scanned the jungle, lingering on the glimpse of aquamarine that marked the lagoon. A resident sea monster, she guessed, before she burst out laughing.

"What's funny?" Shou asked.

Xan fought to regain her composure, waving her hands around. "Just wondering if there's a sea monster living in the lagoon."

Shou shrugged. "When you've had a chance to go diving in there, Ms Lane, you tell me."

The clouds overhead chose that moment to dump a downpour on her head, so Xan sprinted for the shelter of a nearby building, leaving Shou on the landing pad.

Mysteries, a meeting with Meier and maybe even a sea monster — at least today would be different. Xan needed a distraction from the despair threatening to overwhelm her. Romance Island Resort promised to deliver that and more.

FIFTEEN

Phuong breathed a sigh of relief as her car started. Norman had kept her locked in the house for so long, she was scared the battery might have been flat. As it was, she intended to drive as far and as fast as she could away from Norman.

She'd been stupid to waste so much time on a man who only saw her as his slave, someone he kept captive in his house for sex and menial work. She'd have been better off turning to prostitution like Lin had. Norman was right about one thing – all her efforts with him had been useless. She'd been useless. She had two-thirds of a business degree and she hadn't seen a losing deal even when she was in it. Perhaps her brother was right and educating her was a waste of money. How could she possibly save her father's company if she couldn't even negotiate a deal that resulted in her completing her degree?

Two months with Norman that she had nothing to

show for, except some additional cooking skills and the ability to feign interest in sex when she hated the man lying on top of her. She'd lost count of the number of times she'd wanted to vomit in his face instead of submitting to his disgusting rutting. It would be a long time before she wanted to share a bed with any man again.

Well, unless he had the body of a Greek god, like Jason did. She'd make an exception for him.

A mad plan formed in her mind. She'd go find Jason. Drive up to Broome and the resort where he worked and see if he truly was the man he said he was. After talking to him online for so long, she felt like she knew him as no one else did, and she couldn't deny she'd been fantasising about him since he'd first made contact with her. She'd made a mistake with Norman, but now she had a chance to start anew with Jason. University enrolment and the fee payment deadline were only weeks away; all that time she'd wasted with Norman had denied her this semester of study, but if things worked out with Jason, maybe she could enrol next semester. Yes. That's what she'd do.

So she drove and drove and drove some more until dawn blazed on her right, half blinding her. Where was she? She'd been driving between creamy sand dunes for a while now and a sign pointing to a backpackers place guided her to a decision. That's where she'd sleep and when she woke, she could buy a map and keep driving to Broome. It couldn't be that far, surely, she thought as she collapsed on her dormitory bunk.

Oblivion retreated when she heard voices murmuring in a language she didn't know. Her eyes snapped open and she leaped up, bashing her head on the underside of the bed above her. Bunk beds? She'd never shared a room before…before Norman. What she'd have given to be separated from him in bunk beds instead of forced to share his double bed. No more, though. She was free.

The foreign couple stared at her, so she forced a smile and told them she was okay. She shouldered her bag and stumbled out of the room in search of a bathroom.

Some time later, feeling freshened up but starving, she followed her nose to the kitchen. The smell of toast and bacon told her that she'd slept right through the rest of the day and into the next. In the huge communal kitchen, she found the couple who'd woken her.

"Good morning," the girl greeted her with a strong German accent. "I'm Ria and this is Hans." She pointed at the man, who was now sniffing delicately at a sachet of vegemite, the salty Australian spread that Phuong knew was the best hangover cure known to man, if you could keep it down. "We're from Germany and we're travelling around Australia. How about you? Where are you from?"

Phuong licked her lips. Should she say she was Aussie or Singaporean? Which would confuse anyone more if they were following her? Did it matter? "I'm driving up to Broome," she said.

"Would you like company?" Ria offered. "We wanted to visit Broome, but it's so far to drive and the flights are very expensive. We can give you money toward fuel and help you drive, if you like." She added something in German to Hans, who stared at Phuong with interest.

Phuong lowered her eyes under their scrutiny. "That would be nice. I've never been to Broome before. If you have a map and know the way…we could share costs." She didn't have any money — she'd paid for her accommodation with a credit card, too. So stupid. If anyone was following her, all they'd need to do was track transactions. She needed to visit a bank and fill the car with fuel before she left town and disappeared properly. "I'll leave in an hour — meet you here?"

"Sure," Ria said, her friendly smile reassuring Phuong just the tiniest bit. No one would smile that happily if they knew they were driving with a fugitive. Her secret would be safe for a little longer.

SIXTEEN

"Ooh, you must be Ms Lane!" Pale blonde hair framing a pixie-like face, complete with a picture-perfect, pink frangipani tucked behind one ear, captured Xan's attention before she dropped her gaze to the receptionist's name tag.

"Call me Xan, please, Heloise," she replied with a tight smile.

Heloise flashed a set of impossibly white teeth before smothering her giggle. "If you say so, Ms Lane…Xan. None of us were sure how to pronounce your name. Is it short for Alexandra?"

"No." Xan moistened her lips, suddenly wishing she'd had time to tidy herself up, and the drenching downpour hadn't helped matters. She was painfully aware of the difference between backpackers and this resort's elite clientele, and this vision of perfection whose only job was greeting guests brought it firmly into focus. Did all the staff look like they'd stepped out of the pages of a magazine? Would she be expected to do the same? If the resort had a day spa, she needed to book in for everything immediately.

"Ms Lane?"

Xan turned and found herself face to face with Max Meier, to her relief. He didn't look half as polished as Heloise. She hitched her smile back up. "As promised. Thanks for sending a helicopter."

Meier nodded curtly. "With a storm forecast for the weekend, I wasn't taking any chances that the road would be closed. When that happens, flying's the only way in or out of here."

Talk about remote. Xan found herself nodding. She'd heard horror stories about the Cape Leveque Road, though watching the rusty ribbon twist through scrubland as they flew up the peninsula this morning was the closest she'd ever come to travelling along it. "Good to know."

He coughed. "Shall we go to my office?" When Xan nodded again, he led the way and gestured for her to take a seat before he closed the door. His steps were heavy as he crossed the room, his shoulders slumped as if he carried the weight of the world. When he sank into his seat, his knuckles whitened in a death-grip on the chair arms.

He couldn't have had a worse week than hers, Xan mused. She'd never drunk so much bourbon in such a short time. She glanced around at the prints on his walls. There was a photo of him holding a giant fish, but none of anyone else. Maybe Meier didn't have a wife and kids.

Meier pushed a stapled pile of papers across the desk. "Your amended contract." He clicked a pen several times, so it sounded more like a nervous tic than a firm cocking of a favourite weapon, and handed it to Xan.

She set the pen down and perused the pages. At first glance, it looked identical. "Is this the same as the first one you sent?"

"No." Meier leaned across the desk and flipped to the page about her probation period. "There. No probation. You start work on Monday as a permanent employee, once we've both signed the contract." He didn't meet her eyes.

Xan stared at the space no longer occupied by the offending paragraph. A permanent job in paradise. Why did it seem too good to be true?

"What's wrong? Now you've seen the place, you don't want to work here? Is that it?" Meier's eyes held a challenge. "I hope you haven't been wasting my time, Ms Lane."

"No. I've signed all the rest of the paperwork and accepted the position. It's just…a feeling. Isn't there always a snake in paradise?" Xan attempted to smile, but worried that she'd produced a sick grimace instead.

Meier started, then recovered so quickly Xan wondered if she'd imagined it. "We do get some gorgeous sea snakes in the lagoon. Part of living in a tropical paradise." He nodded at the contract. "Aside from the deleted clause, I assure you it's identical to the one I emailed you originally. Are you going to sign it or shall I call the pilot to take you back to the mainland?"

Give up now? Had Meier found someone else he preferred to give the job to, after all the paperwork she'd filled out? No way in hell was she going home now. There was nothing left for her in the UK.

Xan scrawled her signature on the contract, not caring if it was legible or not. "Of course not. I'll see out my contract and when the first year's up, perhaps even extend it. Sea snakes don't scare me, Max. I've swum with sharks and I'll do it again." She pushed the papers back to him.

His breath hissed out and he deflated. She expected him to look defeated, but Meier seemed relieved. Maybe he hadn't wanted someone else in the job, after all, but was being pushed by the owners to take on a different applicant. Too late now – the contract was signed. The position was hers and no one else's.

"So, what now?" Xan prompted.

"You'll start work on Monday morning, as we discussed. Your office and accommodation will be ready for you then, too. In the meantime, I'll get Heloise to arrange a guest room for you in the hotel. You can spend the weekend exploring the island, seeing what we offer our guests, before working on how you can improve on the experience Monday morning." Meier tapped on his computer keyboard. "Meals and everything are included, of course. We have award-winning chefs in our restaurant, as it's what our high-profile clients expect." He rose and offered his hand. "Welcome aboard, Ms Lane."

She shook his clammy hand, then tried to surreptitiously wipe hers on her shorts. Whatever secrets this place held, it had to be better than arguing over ten-dollar forks. As for the frog freak-outs…well, she wouldn't miss the screaming.

SEVENTEEN

Phuong wanted to scream until she ran out of breath.

"We should have stopped at that roadhouse," Hans lamented for what Phuong thought was the third time. She hunched over the steering wheel and kept driving, wishing he'd shut up, but he didn't. "I saw clouds over there and it looked like rain. If we camp, we'll get rained on when that storm comes in. We should go back to the roadhouse."

"The mini one? They only had motel rooms and they were full. Besides, that was over a hundred kilometres back. Those clouds were in the east. Everyone knows the weather comes in from the west here. We're better off camping, Hans. Where's your sense of adventure?" Ria's enthusiasm was almost as grating, Phuong decided. "We should stop soon. There's a bridge ahead. That means a river. That would be a good place to camp."

Phuong rubbed her eyes and managed to discern the

bridge in the distance. She couldn't see much in the way of water beneath it, but she did need rest. Not to mention Hans and Ria would hopefully be silent while they slept.

Sleepily, she followed Ria's directions as the girl pointed to a track that led from the road down to the dry river bed. She didn't follow the track, though — her little hatchback wasn't a four-wheel-drive and the steep incline didn't look like something her car could handle. She mumbled something to that effect and Ria nodded cheerfully as they ground to a halt in the gravel beside the road.

Not for the first time, Phuong wondered if the girl was on some kind of drugs. No one could possibly be that happy all the time.

Hans continued moaning about camping in the rain until Ria agreed to set up camp under the bridge, in the dry river bed. Well, almost dry. Hans had sounded almost venomous when he shouted back that there was water in the river. A trickle, but it was still water.

Phuong leaned against her car until Ria shouldered her last bag and headed down the incline with it. With no camping gear to speak of and only a small bag of clothes to her name, Phuong intended to sleep in the car, where snakes and all manner of creepy crawlies couldn't get to her. Camping was for crazy backpackers.

Sighing, she pushed the driver's seat as far back as it would go and pulled out her phone. She hadn't checked her email since she'd left Norman's flat, even though she'd heard the trill of incoming messages in Geraldton.

The first one she clicked on was from Jason. He'd taken a picture of himself in some kid's inflatable boat, so small his legs stuck over the side, centimetres above clear water that was teeming with what looked like baby sharks. Whatever they were, they weren't much bigger than his feet. Beneath the picture, he'd written: "Maybe you're a little mermaid and that's why you haven't given me your answer? Pick up your shell-phone, sexy siren. Save me from this shark-infested shipwreck so we can live happily ever after."

For the first time in days, she smiled. If her phone had had a signal, she'd have replied on the spot with a resounding yes. She wanted to shout it so loud that her voice rolled across the scrubby desert vegetation, all the way across the sea to his lonely island. Where she'd join him soon.

Cuddling her phone to her chest, Phuong sank into sleep. Everything would be better in the morning.

EIGHTEEN

For a long time, Xan stared at the tiny bottle of bourbon from the hotel's mini-bar. It wasn't big enough to deaden the pain tonight. She'd have to go to the bar if that's what she wanted. Hauling herself to her feet, Xan peered at her reflection. Bloodshot eyes and a red nose from crying too much. Jerome didn't deserve a single tear from her, but she'd shed thousands in the nights since she'd learned of his betrayal. The cowardly bastard hadn't even tried to apologise – he hadn't called or emailed or even sent her a damn text message. Did he know how many hot men she'd turned down during her trip? A veritable army of Flying Frog Men. Being faithful to that faithless toad. She could've had hot sex every night of the week instead of just imagining it.

Xan burst out laughing. As if she'd ever done that. When she'd slept with Jerome, it had been short and sweet, that's all. Hot sex was the stuff of the battered books left behind at the backpackers. One-night stands weren't something she'd ever done. Why start now?

Because the biggest bastard in Britain had broken her heart and for this weekend, she was just another anonymous guest in paradise.

For a moment, she considered it. Going to a pub to shag a sexy stranger? Why the hell not?

She washed her face in the basin, scrubbing at her skin until all traces of tears were washed away. No amount of concealer could hide the dark circles under her eyes, but bars didn't have the brightest lighting, anyway. A bit of bright lipstick and swapping her shirt and shorts for her little black dress would do, surely.

Her heels ticked on the tiled floor as she made her way down the corridor, past Reception and into the bar. The Jungle, it was called, and the potted palms scattered around made it look like the vegetation outside. Weaving her way through tables and trees, Xan found the place surprisingly empty for a Friday night. Not like the Roebuck Hotel or Divers Tavern back in Broome — the bar at either of those would be crowded three or four deep by now, yet she stood alone at this one, with the bartender's full attention.

"What can I get you?" he asked easily.

A whole bottle of bourbon, she thought but didn't say. Drinking herself under the table wasn't the best way to seduce a man, or not the sort she wanted, anyway. Xan raised her eyes to the menu on the wall.

"You know your first drink's free, don't you? Your warm welcome to the resort?"

Xan didn't, but she wasn't sure that applied to her,

anyway. "I'll have a beer. What do you have?"

The barman grinned. "The best beer we have here is local. Once you've tasted it, you won't want anything else. I'll start you off with a mango – "

"No!" Xan interrupted. "If you have Matso's, I'll take the ginger. With plenty of ice."

The barman raised an eyebrow. "Not your first time here, then." He jerked his chin. "ID."

Xan almost laughed. Did he think she was under eighteen? He wasn't laughing, though, so she fumbled for her wallet.

"Not that kind." He tapped his wrist, or, more accurately, the oversized digital watch he wore. "Your resort ID."

"Oh!" Xan unclipped her matching wristband and held it out. "Sorry."

The barman hesitated before he finally took it. The scanner pad beeped and he handed the watch back, his eyes on the screen. "You're...you're Ms Lane?"

"Yes."

He straightened and held out his hand. "I'm sorry, I thought you'd be older. I'm Marcel. Mostly I work the bar, but my speciality is hen's parties." He winked. "I'm a very skilled dancer. Those nights...I'm Magic Marcel."

Xan blinked. Blushed. Blinked again. She'd never met a man so proud to admit he was a stripper. Then again, she'd seen the queue that night the Sun Cinemas had screened the latest *Magic Mike* movie. "Call me Xan," she replied, shaking his hand. "Is it normally this quiet?" She waved her free hand at the empty bar.

He shrugged. "It's dinner time in the wet season. Most

guests are still in the restaurant. When they close, everyone moves here, but with the races on, most people are in town for the weekend."

The races? How could she have forgotten? If she'd still been working at the backpackers, she'd have been trackside with most of the guests. Most of town, too, admittedly. She'd never been a big fan of horse racing back in the UK, but here in Broome, with the red dirt track, it was a far cry from the turf at home.

Marcel set her drink on a tray. "You're welcome to sit at the bar, but the best spot tonight is out on the veranda, overlooking the ocean." He grabbed the tray and walked away.

Xan slid off her barstool and followed him. He placed her drink on a dimly-lit table by the veranda railing.

"If there's a storm, you'll see lightning and waves, but if the clouds clear up, you get a sky full of stars." Marcel leaned out over the railing and pointed. "The rain's stopped and the moon's rising over there in a few hours, so I think you're in for the Milky Way tonight." He glanced back. "Enjoy it." He returned to the bar, where a well-dressed couple waited to be served.

Xan sat back, sipping her drink, as she watched the bar patrons instead of the sky.

They entered in pairs, dressed for a fancy dinner and not a night at the pub, and the only single men were her father's age or older. Business executives or whatever they were, they weren't her type. No, if Xan intended to throw away her principles for a night, it would be with some hot young stud, not a silver fox who'd expect her to fulfil his fantasies.

Oh no – she'd looked too long. A man who looked fifty,

if he was a day, flashed her welcoming smile and gestured toward the empty seat across from him. Xan blushed and shook her head. He raised his whisky glass in a toast to her before his eyes darted elsewhere.

Allowing herself to breathe again, Xan kept her eyes on the darkness outside, where the stars had started to appear. Well, mostly planets at first, she figured, wishing she knew more about Southern Hemisphere constellations. Hey, that was something she could put on her list of activities for the hotel – stargazing.

"You can't see a fucking thing from there," drawled a voice in the darkness.

Xan peered out to find the source of the voice, but he was right about one thing – she couldn't see him. She could hear the approaching footsteps, though, as the voice's owner ascended the veranda steps and strode across the deck.

Now, she could see everything not covered by his board shorts, which was the only clothing the man wore. Not that he needed to cover up a body that rivalled that of the Flying Frog Man. What she could see of it, anyway.

He swigged from a half-full bottle of bourbon, slammed it down on her table, and wiped his mouth on his forearm. Judging by his unsteady gait, the rest of the bourbon was already sloshing through his bloodstream. He flashed a grin. "You're new, and you're hot, too."

Hands down, Bourbon Boy was the youngest bloke present. Definitely the only one under thirty, except maybe the barman. But Xan had no intention of settling for less than stellar if it came to sex.

"Who isn't? The wet season in Broome's humid and hot

as hell. Hence why I'm drinking." She lifted her glass to her lips and sipped the liquid that remained. Mostly melted ice, but that didn't matter.

"You're out." Bourbon Boy snapped his fingers. "Oi, Marcel. Lady here needs another."

Xan turned in time to see the irritation on Marcel's face before he nodded and ducked beneath the counter. In no time at all, the smiling barman brought her a second drink. "Here you are, Ms…Xan. I'll put in the drinks order on Monday morning, so let me know if you'd like the distributor to put another case on the truck for you. We only get a delivery once a fortnight in wet season, you see, so if we run out, it could be another three weeks before we get any more."

Three weeks for more beer? They really were in the middle of nowhere out here. She thanked Marcel, who frowned at Bourbon Boy before returning to the bar.

The bottle of bourbon upended, glugging down the man's throat. An amber stream trickled from the side of his mouth, down the ridges of his sculpted chest and abs. He caught her staring and grinned. "Well, Zzzzan. I'm Jay. Come with me. I'll get you closer to the stars than you ever thought possible." He grabbed her hand in his free one and tugged.

"My drink?"

"Bring it!"

She barely had time to seize the ginger beer bottle before Jay yanked her out of her seat. With his fierce grip on her hand, she had no choice but to follow him down the stairs and into the dark.

"Where are you taking me?" she demanded, trying

valiantly to free herself.

"Relax, Zzzzan. We're not leaving the island. I'm taking you to the private Penguin jetty." He bumped the bourbon bottle against his wristband. "Your tracker will keep you safe. Hotel security are watching your every move. Plus a panic button if you need help. Just tap it and security will come rescue you."

What? Xan glanced at her wristband, but it was too dark to see much of it. It was her ID and room key, she knew, but a tracking device? It was as big as those deluxe diving watches in the dive shop in town, so the wristband could hold a GPS, but the expense of handing them out to every guest…

"Wouldn't do to lose a VIP, sweetheart. Want me to show you the stars like you've never seen them before?" Bourbon Boy – Jay – took another unsteady step on the path.

How much trouble could she get into, anyway? This was paradise and her new home.

"Sure."

NINETEEN

Phuong woke up with cold feet. Not just cold, either — soaking wet. That couldn't be right. She jumped up and bumped her head on the ceiling, a painful reminder that she was in her car. Where there shouldn't be any water. Peering down, she saw dark water swirling in the footwell. How on Earth....

She glanced out the window, scanning the scene that seemed even more unbelievable in the pre-dawn light. Her car sat in a shallow stream so wide that she couldn't see the other side — or the bridge she'd crossed last night. As the light brightened, she realised what she was seeing wasn't a stream at all, but the return of the river that hadn't been home last night. Somehow, water upstream had come flooding down here and it was already over the wheels of her car. If she didn't get out of there quickly, she'd be swept away, car and all.

Phuong wrenched her key in the ignition, praying to anyone who'd listen that her engine would work. By some miracle, it coughed into life. She shoved the car into gear, slamming her foot into the puddle to floor the accelerator. When she reached dry road, she slowed the car to a stop and burst into tears. She'd come so close to dying in that flood. Good thing she hadn't slept under the bridge with those two backpackers, who…

Her heart plummeted. Hans and Ria.

She twisted around in her seat, peering back at the way she'd come, but there was no sign of them. Their camp site had been obliterated by the raging river while she slept. There was nothing she could do – she didn't have a car that could go off-road, and she didn't have any rope to pull them to safety, even if she found them. Her best bet was to drive to the next roadhouse and ask for help there.

Grimly, she ground her car into gear and sped away from the torrent that had taken her travelling companions. What else could go wrong?

TWENTY

After a moment, Xan forced Jay to stop so she could slip off her heels. Clutching her shoes and her drink to her chest with her free arm, Xan trotted beside him, their bare feet slapping on the faintly lit path through the jungle.

Waves crashed, leaves rustled and something swooped between the trees overhead, but Xan couldn't see any of it clearly. Even the stars above only appeared between the gaps of the palm tree canopy turning the path into a tunnel of sorts. But a tunnel to where?

"Where are we going?" Xan demanded.

"I told you. The private Penguin jetty."

"What the hell does that mean?"

"It's a jetty and it's private and it has no lights, so it's the best place to look at the stars." Jay pointed into the darkness ahead, where the lights ended. "There."

"What about the private penguins?" None of this made

sense.

"There aren't any. It's the wet season and we're the only ones here. Not that anyone ever comes here. Guests don't stay in Villa Penguin. You can come here whenever you want." Jay dragged her further into the dark.

This was stupid. Xan fished out her phone and held it up so she could see where she was going. To her surprise, he was right — before them was a wooden jetty extending out over midnight-coloured waves, though it wasn't even nine o'clock yet, according to her phone. Too early to be doing crazy stuff.

Her feet didn't agree with her, though. They kept walking, even when the paved path ended in damp wooden boards. She should turn around and go to bed — alone.

"Now lie down," Jay ordered.

Xan burst out laughing. As if! First the arrogant prick had dragged her all the way out here without explaining why or where, and now he thought he could demand sex? "Screw you."

"Maybe later, babe, but I'm gonna do the stars first. First clear night in ages." He threw his empty bourbon bottle over the waves and stretched out at the end of the jetty, folding his hands behind his head. "And turn that fucking phone off. Can't see as much when there's lights on."

She stared at him. He really wanted to stare at the stars? And here she'd thought it was a euphemism for…something. She tucked her phone away. Sighing, she settled on the jetty, sipped her drink, and lifted her eyes. Wow, the weirdo was right. With the lights off and her vision adjusting to the darkness, she could see millions of stars, like a spray of glitter across the whole damn sky.

Sitting cross-legged and twisting her neck around to look straight up wasn't the most comfortable way to do this, though…

Xan glanced at Jay, who was too intent on the sky to notice her anymore.

So much for seduction or a one night stand. Stars it would be. Safer, too. She set her empty bottle down.

Scooting her bum along the jetty to put more distance between Jay's body and hers, Xan lay back and looked up. What she'd thought was a cloud at first resolved into a thousand tiny pinpricks, each a sun so far away she'd never seen it before. Light flared on the edge of her vision. She turned her head just in time to see something streak across the sky before it vanished.

"Did you see that?" she and Jay said at the same time.

"You have to make a wish for shooting stars," Xan added, fervently wishing to succeed in her role at the resort.

"That's bullshit," Jay grunted. "Wishes don't come true, and all the fairy tales your parents told you as a kid are the biggest lie of all."

Xan wasn't sure what to respond with. What could you say?

"You make plans, but they all go to shit. I loved her for years. Since primary school. Knew we'd be together one day. I just had to be patient and wait, so we'd have our happy ending." Jay laughed harshly. "But she had other ideas for Prince Charming. Rapist bastard."

What? Xan sat up. "Who?"

"Prince Charming, of course. The fucker had his way with Sleeping Beauty. That's what woke her up. She should've threatened him with a knife."

Xan said lightly, "That's not the Disney story I remember."

"Cartoons for kids. Nothing like real life. She picked the one who hurt her and threatened me. I'd never hurt her. Never. But she's marrying the violent bastard. I tried to protect her from him. I did. No thank you, though. No, she's going to marry him and I have to leave the fucking country..." Jay's voice dropped too low for her to understand, though Xan hadn't understood much of his rambling.

Xan ignored him and watched for more shooting stars. She could do with another wish or two. Or...

A flurry of lights flared and vanished like a cloud of sparks in the sky. Enough for more wishes than she could think of.

She wished her parents would stay safe and healthy while she was here.

That she'd solve the resort's mysteries.

That Jerome's dick would fall off.

That she'd get her own happy ending one day and it would be nothing like Jay's bitter ramblings. Nothing like Jay at all.

Xan glanced at Jay, who'd fallen silent. "Jay?"

He let out a loud snore.

Oh, how charming. No wonder his princess had chosen Prince Charming over him.

Xan rose and made her way back to the lit path. Better to go to bed alone than to make a mistake with a man she barely knew.

"Maybe not, baby," she whispered.

Jay snored on, oblivious, while she headed back to her

hotel room.

TWENTY-ONE

Phuong crept across the third flooded section of road, hoping that the water wasn't too deep to cross. Warning signs on both sides of the road told of the dangers of being swept away – as if she needed the reminder. Hans and Ria might be dead now and she'd nearly joined them.

Her tyres made a crunching sound instead of the swish of travelling through the creek, and Phuong let out a breath she hadn't known she'd been holding. She couldn't stop, though. She had to continue to the next roadhouse to tell them what had happened so they'd send help.

She just had to keep going. Over a bridge that rose out of yet another brown torrent, but this river hadn't reached the top of the bridge yet. She sped across the bridge and almost cried when the roadhouse came into view as she rounded the bend.

For a place in the middle of nowhere, it sure was a

popular spot. Cars, trucks and caravans were parked everywhere except at the petrol pumps. People filled the shop, spilling out onto the veranda and even queueing on the paving outside. While she waited for the crowd to disperse, Phuong filled her car with fuel, figuring that she'd need it for the long round trip to the river and back. The throng didn't thin, so she joined the end of the line and settled in for a long wait.

After what felt like forever, she finally made it inside the shop, where the privileged few had access to air conditioning and a TV tuned to the morning news. The news anchor frowned as she described flooding and road closures throughout the Gascoyne. The pictures on TV cut to yellow barriers on what looked like the road outside – yes, they were outside, she realised, peering through the dusty glass. She wouldn't be able to return for Hans and Ria until the road reopened. Phuong turned back to the news report, hoping to hear when that might be, but the programme had already moved to another news story – a missing persons report.

Phuong gasped as her own face occupied the screen. "If you see Fiona, please contact police or encourage her to make herself known – "

She had to get out of there before anyone recognised her, but her legs had turned to jelly. She couldn't go back to Norman. Wouldn't go back to the life of a slave. Slowly, Phuong forced her feet to take one step, then another, slipping between the queuing customers to the warm, dusty air outside. Her hands shook as she unlocked her car and slid the keys into the ignition, but she had to go.

Shoving the car into gear, Phuong headed for the

highway, hoping no one had seen her or if they had, that they hadn't recognised her. She had to get to Jason and his island paradise. For all Jason's jokes, she'd need a knight in shining armour to save her from Norman.

TWENTY-TWO

This was paradise. No question about it. Two days spent drinking in the bar, lazing on the beach in between downpours, snorkelling in the lagoon, getting thoroughly thrashed at beach volleyball by a woman twice her age, moaning in delight at the restaurant chef's magical creations at mealtimes…by Monday morning, Xan didn't want to leave Romance Island Resort. She was thoroughly in love with the place. She hadn't seen Jay since Friday night, but that was fine by her. She didn't want to build a reputation for sleeping with guests, however well-built they might be. Some of those older guys might get ideas…

Xan laughed into the shower spray. For the first time since Jerome's betrayal, she felt hope for the future. Oh, sure, she still wanted to rip his balls off and watch him choke on them while he bled to death, but she'd managed a whole two hours without fantasising about it. That was progress, right there.

Admittedly, she had been snorkelling through the shark nursery at the time, and the thought of a thousand hungry baby sharks shredding the flesh from his bones while he screamed had provided quite a distraction, but...

She had to hurry or she'd be late for work. She'd spent too long stressing over what to wear on her first day. Casual or formal business attire? After all, a tour guide could be doing anything from diving through to meeting and greeting VIPs. In the end, the humidity had won. She'd chosen a business skirt, but paired it with a sleeveless top. Xan packed her belongings back into her suitcase in anticipation of moving to her official accommodation during the morning. She hesitated when she reached her suit jacket, the one that matched her skirt. It was too hot to wear, but if circumstances required it...Xan threw the jacket over her arm and wheeled her suitcase out behind her, hoping she looked as put-together as possible.

"Checking out?" the man at Reception greeted her.

"Sort of," Xan replied. "I've been staying in the hotel, but I start work this morning, so it looks like the luxury part of my stay is over and it's time to shift to the staff accommodation. I'm Xan Lane."

He shook her hand. "Toby. Usually I split the night porter shifts with Dan here, but I sort of got conscripted into doing day shift today, what with –" he coughed "– everything and all." He stared at the computer for a moment before he added, "Hey, Dan, can you take her to her new place?"

Dan, who'd just reached the outside door, turned and nodded. "Sure, if Housekeeping are done cleaning. Pamela said she was doing it first thing this morning."

Before Dan was done speaking, Toby had the phone to his ear, nodding as he spoke to someone called Annette. After less than a minute, he hung up again. "Yeah, Pamela's done. Should be safe to go through."

Dan held the door and Xan hurried to follow him, dragging her luggage.

"Let me get that," he said after a moment, relieving her of the bag. "We lost a bit of the decking in the last cyclone, so it'll be a rough ride for the wheels until we get it fixed. Maintenance are on it, though. Just waiting for the supply truck to get through the road closures."

Xan found herself nodding as Dan pointed out the staff dining room, communal bathroom facilities and individual staff bedrooms in what looked more like mining accommodation dongas than buildings at a prestigious hotel. They made the rooms at Broome Backpackers look palatial by comparison. She hadn't considered she might be worse off than she'd been in the house she'd shared in town with a couple of tour guides. Single beds and cramped quarters…

Mentally, she shook herself. She'd stayed in worse. Her flat back home, for a start. All she had to do in her room was sleep here – when she wasn't working, she could spend every spare minute making the most of living in paradise.

Dan bumped her suitcase up some steps to a veranda where the doors were more widely spaced. He stopped at the one on the end. "You'll need your ID."

Hesitantly, Xan lifted her wristband to the scanner, which beeped before the door clicked.

Dan twisted the handle and opened the door for her,

waiting for Xan to precede him before he brought her bag in. "I'm buggered, so I'm going to bed, unless you need anything else?" When Xan shook her head, he gave her a tired nod and ambled away.

Xan let her breath out in a relieved hiss. Instead of a box she could barely move in, she stood in the living area of a flat bigger than the one she'd had at home. Kitchen, couch, TV and even a dining table fitted comfortably in it. She peered through a doorway and found a bedroom with an ensuite bathroom visible through another open door. For a one bedroom flat, it dwarfed the bedsit she'd had back home.

But she had work to do, so after dragging her bag to the bedroom, Xan returned to Reception.

She caught Toby's eye. "Ah, Max mentioned I had an office?"

"Max? Oh, Mr Meier. Right. He said we had to call him that in front of guests, because he was the manager and all. Yeah, your office is through here. Heloise said the paperwork and your temporary passwords would be on the desk, waiting for you." He led the way down the corridor to an office Xan could've sworn was the one Meier had taken her to on Friday, but both he and his photographed fish were gone. The place looked sterile.

"So is it Heloise's day off? What do you do here on your days off? Is there a fly-in-fly-out arrangement with shifts like the mine sites?"

Toby coughed. "Not really. We usually catch the carrier boat to the pearl farm and drive to town from there. The resort keeps a couple of four-wheel-drives on the mainland, but most of the staff park our cars at the farm, too.

Heloise…she doesn't work here any more."

Xan stopped. Heloise hadn't acted like a disgruntled employee when Xan saw her at Reception over the weekend. Even yesterday afternoon, she'd seen the girl chatting at length with one of the guests. "Why not? What happened?"

"Yesterday she was out of uniform on Reception." Toby licked his lips, his eyes darting around to look at anything but Xan.

"And it's instant dismissal for anyone not seen in public areas in full uniform? Sounds a bit draconian, if you ask me." Xan waited until Toby met her eyes. "If this is some sort of prank you play on new staff, don't bother. Oh, and I know all about the local dropbears, too. I used to run the backpackers in town. What happened with Heloise?"

Toby crept to the corridor, peered around, then quietly closed the door. His dropped to a whisper, "It's not a joke. She was out of uniform on Reception. Wearing nothing but that pink flower, twined around some naked guest on the desk. Some guests walked in on them and…well, they asked to see the manager. Mr Meier didn't really have much choice. They left in the same helicopter yesterday."

Right. No having sex in the hotel foyer in front of the guests. Xan could see how that could be a fireable offence. Not that she ever intended to. The rest of Toby's words sank in. "So Meier's not here?"

"Er, no," Toby replied slowly, as if that was obvious. He waved at the stack of papers on the desk. "But he left all that for you. You should be good, he said."

Xan smiled broadly. Yes. Yes, she would. "We'll see, I guess." With no boss to report to, this was going to be an interesting day. What if she had questions? "Do you know when he'll be back?"

Toby laughed. "Well, never. At least, that's what he said. That's why you're here. The new hotel manager."

"Wait...I'm what, sorry?"

Xan reached for the stack of papers and found her signed contract. She leafed feverishly through the pages until she found the bit about her job title and duties. It was right there, in black and white: HOTEL MANAGER, not Tours and Activities Manager, like she'd applied for. And she'd signed the damn thing without a protest.

TWENTY-THREE

Incessant banging startled Phuong from a sound sleep and made her peer through her dust-caked windows in panic. A demon in a small boy's body grinned at her, drummed on her car one more time and skipped off happily at having raised hell. No one else was in sight, though the road trains she'd parked between had since left, and the sun was high in the sky. The roadhouse was open now, which meant she could get more fuel and be on her way. Driving this far made her car slurp fuel like fish drank water. Hundreds of kilometres every day until she reached her final destination. How much longer to go?

Which roadhouse was this? Phuong craned her neck to read the sign. Sandfire. If she'd read the map right, this was the last roadhouse before the turnoff to Broome. Some time this afternoon, she'd be able to stop running. And maybe, just maybe, she'd be safe. But she had to get there first.

She started her car and trundled to the fuel pumps, then stiffly got out. Tonight, she'd sleep in a bed and not her car, she swore. Flexing her fingers, she tried to work out the cramps from her death grip on the steering wheel, but still her hands ached. Even holding the pump handle hurt. Finally, the fuel tank was full. Phuong shook the pump to extract the last few drops before sealing the tank that was her ticket to Broome.

She staggered in to the shop, counting out cash to cover her fuel. A display of discount chocolate bars caught her eye. When had he last eaten or drunk anything? She dumped a handful of random snacks on the counter as her stomach rumbled its approval. It wasn't enough, though - her dry mouth tasted like a rat had nested in it. She grabbed a bottle of water and added it to the pile.

The shop assistant barely glanced at her. She told Phuong the total, checked the cash and deposited it in the till with a disinterest Phuong could have kissed her for, but she didn't. Instead, she bundled her purchases in her arms and carried them out to her car.

Ripping open a chocolate bar, she shoved it into her mouth as she returned to the highway, raising a cloud of red dust in her wake. When she saw a sign proclaiming that it was only 325 kilometres to Broome, she cheered so loud she almost choked. Less than half a day's drive and she'd be home. Funny how a place she'd never seen could be home, but when you had nothing else...

Jason. She had to find Jason. Wherever he was would be safe and home.

TWENTY-FOUR

"Mr Meier!" As if Xan's morning wasn't already mad enough, a man wearing a khaki safari shirt and shorts burst into her office. "Mr Meier, he's done it again. It's worse than ever. He won't move, either. You've got to –" He caught sight of Xan and stopped dead. "Where's Mr Meier?"

Toby coughed. "Ah, Lee, this is Xan Lane, the new manager. Mr Meier's replacement."

Xan wanted to strangle the man, but he was only stating the truth, at least as he saw it. This mess wasn't the night porter's fault. She summoned her most serene smile. Never mind that she had to grit her teeth and think about feeding the man responsible to the sharks in the lagoon in order to produce something more believable than a grimace.

Lee eyed her nervously. "I work in Maintenance and someone logged a fault with the spa. When I went over to investigate…" His eyes beseeched her to believe him. "He was lying there unconscious. I can't wake him and I can't get him to move."

A medical emergency she could handle, or at least she hoped so. "Lead the way," Xan commanded.

Lee skittered out of the office and broke into a trot when they left the office. Xan jogged to keep up as he led her past the gym and into what the sign said was the health club. Some health club – all she could see was a spa in a big pavilion, surrounded by decking and sun lounges.

"He's there." Lee pointed at a clump of potted palms.

Xan peered around the decorative trees. Oh, God. She was profoundly glad she hadn't had breakfast yet. A near-naked man lay on the decking in a pool of what looked and smelled like vomit. It was like being back at the backpackers all over again. Only last week she'd had to deal with some drunken twenty-year-old who'd discovered Australia's eighteen-plus drinking age at about the same time as he'd tried to drink Divers Tavern dry. Well, she had a bloody procedure for dealing with drunks.

"Get me a bucket."

Lee vanished and returned with two, which he presented proudly. Xan took them both and headed for the spa. When they were both filled with tepid water, she dumped the contents of one on Mr Drunk and Disgusting.

As predicted, he came up spluttering, but Xan had another bucket in reserve in case he turned violent. This time, she didn't need it – he glared blearily at her before sagging back to the decking. "Fuck off."

Xan handed her empty bucket to Lee and gestured for him to refill it while she advanced on the drunk with the full one. This time, she deliberately poured it over his head.

"Fuck off!" the man roared, sitting up. "I'll see you fired for this." He glared at Xan and her heart stopped. The drunk was Jay, minus his bourbon.

"No, you won't. I'm the manager of the hotel. No one here has the authority to fire me." At least, she hoped so.

"Fucking can." He picked up a battered-looking pink frangipani and twirled it between his fingers before throwing it down. Jay squinted at her. "You're new. Have I fucked you yet? Gotta do that first." He tugged at the waistband of his shorts.

Xan took a deep breath. Fury burned through her bones, but her voice was level. "You don't have a snowball's chance in hell, so better keep your pants on, mate. If you don't get up now – and I mean right now – and take your hangover to the privacy of your hotel room, I'll have you removed from the island. This is a resort. The other guests who want to use the health club should be able to do so without having to see this."

Lee sidled over. "Ms Lane, you can't make him leave. Mr Meier tried that, but he just comes back. You can't keep him off the island. He owns the hotel."

Jay's smug smile told her he'd heard every word.

Thank heaven she'd thought to get that probation clause removed from her contract, though she thought she knew why Meier had agreed to it. The bastard didn't want her skipping out when she discovered that he'd bolted. Well, she'd be pushing her luck to the limit today. "Really? So that makes you staff. Well, let me introduce myself. I'm Xan Lane, the new manager at Romance Island Resort. If you ever, and I mean ever, suggest that I have sex with you, I'll report you for sexual harassment. And if that flower's any evidence to go by, I won't be the only one. I'll call the receptionist, Heloise, and see if she has a complaint to make."

Jay grinned and winked. "Baby, no woman who spends the night with me has anything to complain about."

Those eyes, the shit-eating grin she wanted to wipe off with a well-placed foot…Xan gasped. She knew him and not just from that night on the jetty. He'd cut his hair, so she hadn't recognised him at first. This was the arrogant ass who'd been lording it over his harem in Matso's, all those months ago. What was his name? Jay…Jay Felix! If this man was his boss, no wonder Meier had left. But if she wanted to stay in Australia, she couldn't quit. That meant gaining the upper hand over this arsehole rock star and never giving an inch. Thank heaven she hadn't done anything but stare at the stars with him on Friday night.

"Mr Felix, go home. You've made a spectacle of yourself, but that's your job, isn't it? Well, running the hotel is mine. So while you go hole up with whoever your current companion is, I have work to do." She turned to wide-eyed Lee. "Can you help Mr Felix home, please?"

"Jay. It's Jay," he insisted, glaring at her. Finally, she'd gotten through to him. Well, irritated him, at least.

Good. She wanted him to dislike her so much he went to wherever his real home was. Anywhere but here, because Xan intended to stay. It was either that or go home, where she'd be forced to see Jerome and Kelly every day. She'd settle in hell first.

Xan watched Jay stagger to his feet and stumble drunkenly away from the health club, Lee dogging his heels but not daring to speak to the man. Awe for an arsehole. Jay didn't deserve it, no matter how many hotels he owned.

Shaking her head, Xan trudged back to her office. She'd managed the backpackers without any problem and she'd been damn good at it. Good enough to land this job, that's for sure. How much harder could managing a resort be?

TWENTY-FIVE

"Romance Island Resort? That's the celebrity place up in the Buccaneer Archipelago. Your best bet's to go to the airport and hire a helicopter," the woman in the Broome Visitor Centre said, eyeing Phuong's dusty clothes as if she knew the girl could barely afford a bus fare, let alone a whole helicopter.

"Isn't there a boat?" Phuong asked weakly.

"The supply boat the staff use from the pearl farm, yeah." The woman nodded as if everything made sense now. "Are you starting work at the resort? I heard they were in need of staff with the dry season not far off."

"Maybe. I'm supposed to meet someone who works there." Phuong pushed the map across the counter. "Can you show me on this how to drive to the boat dock?"

The woman shrugged. "Sure, but you'll need a four-wheel-drive and that's only if the road's open. There's been some flooding with the recent storms."

"Tell me about it. I've driven up from Geraldton. I didn't know the highway was closed until after I got to the barrier at this end. Flooded rivers, roads…it can't be as bad as I've already driven through."

"If you say so." She pointed at the map with her pen. "Now, you're here, so you follow this road until you hit the highway, then head north east until you get to the turnoff with all the signs. Turn left there. Follow it for a couple hundred kilometres until you see the pearl farm on the right. The boat schedule depends on the tides, but the skipper lives at the farm, so they'll know when the next one leaves."

Wanting nothing more than to burst into tears at the thought that she was still hours from her destination, Phuong thanked the woman and dragged herself back to her car.

For a moment, she considered spending the night in a hotel…or, more likely, a cheap backpackers dorm, because that was all she could afford. But the siren call of Jason waiting for her was too much to bear. She couldn't stop now. If she kept going, she'd get to meet him tonight.

Smoothing the map out on the passenger seat, Phuong gunned the engine and set off for what she hoped was the final leg of her trip. A couple hundred kilometres was nothing — she'd driven more than twice that most afternoons. And Jason was at the end of it. How could she even think of delaying?

Romance Island Resort, here I come, she thought, stomping on the accelerator.

Houses quickly gave way to pindan scrub once more.

Broome retreated into memory as little more than a rust-tinted dream. Just a little longer and she'd be safe.

The promised turnoff appeared, signposted with more warnings than she'd ever seen before. Crocodiles, fires, cows…they whizzed past before she'd had time to read more than half of them. If she did, she knew they'd only frighten her. She'd driven this far – how much worse could it get? It's not like she intended to stop now.

Nothing could be worse than what she'd endured already. Phuong was certain of that.

Grimly, she pushed her protesting car to the speed limit, then a little past it for good measure. Her tyres ate up the road as the afternoon light tinted the road gold, then red like the rusty ramparts on either side. The car jolted, its tyres grinding as if she'd driven off the road and onto the gravel siding, but she was still firmly on the road. A glance in her rear-view mirror showed the dusty, bitumen ribbon trailing off into the distance, so she followed the unsealed dirt track it had become. Her teeth jarred as the car bounced and juddered across endless ridges of hard-packed red dirt.

Soon, a cloud of dust obscured the road behind her. Phuong could only go forward as fast as she dared, feeling like her car and her very bones would be shaken apart by the rippled road.

Red dust in front and rust-cloud behind – if there was a road to hell, this looked like it. No, a road out of hell, she promised herself. A road to paradise, if such a place existed. Jason told her it did, and that he lived there. Damn it, she'd seen pictures. Those photos of the beach…

A sharp crack jolted through the car, so it skidded off its

straight path and into the middle of the road. Yanking at the steering wheel, Phuong tried to force her sluggish car back to the left hand side where it belonged, but it didn't seem to want to listen. The car shuddered again and slowed, slewing toward the mound of dust marking the border between road and bush. She felt rather than heard the side of the car scrape against the sandy barrier, but she couldn't seem to pull away. Instead, she was losing speed as the dust dragged her to a halt.

No. She couldn't stop here. Her car couldn't give up here.

Phuong threw open the door and lurched to her feet. She inhaled a lungful of dust and found herself coughing instead of shouting at her car for quitting now, when they were so close.

Her car canted over on one side, as if there was a ditch below the dust rampart, but Phuong couldn't see any ditch, not even when she crouched down and tried to peer under the car. No, it looked like both the tyres on the passenger side were flat and the car now rested on the wheel rims on that side. Phuong had never changed a car tyre in her life and even if she had, she didn't have two spares. Only one, maybe.

She sank to her knees in the dirt. What to do? Should she stay with the car and hope someone else drove down the gritty track, someone kind enough to give her a lift to her destination?

Who would be crazy enough to attempt this road? It had no street lights, no bitumen, and the sun was slowly sinking out of sight. And what if the next car was a police car, come to cart her back to Perth and...Norman...

Phuong forced herself to her feet. If the choice was back to hell or forward into the future, she'd take the future on foot if she had to. Gritting her teeth, she hefted her bag onto her shoulder and pocketed the car keys. Her car might be a quitter, but she wasn't.

What more could this stupid road throw at her? Cows? Crocodiles? Ha! She'd turn their skin into shoes before she'd let anything else get between her and Jason.

TWENTY-SIX

Two days. It took Xan two very dull days of skimming through paperwork before she felt she truly had a handle on resort operations. Profit margins were slim because expensive luxury resorts weren't in as high demand during the recent economic slump. The mining industry downturn hadn't helped matters. Fewer guests could afford the place, but rising costs meant they couldn't drop the fancy price tag.

As for the rising costs…she could lay a lot of them firmly at Jay's door, wherever it was. Since he'd first arrived at the resort, staff turnover rates had reached a record high. One week, they'd lost ten staff – and eight of those were new hires who'd only started work that week. Smelling a rat, Xan had checked the personnel files. Sure enough, the staff were all women under thirty who'd been dismissed for fraternisation. Further research through the hotel's intranet revealed a fraternisation policy...or more accurately, a policy that said there was to be no such thing between staff and anyone on the island. The policy had been changed exactly one week after Jay's arrival, the same day as the previous activities manager had resigned.

A meeting with the human resources officer had been illuminating. One of Jay's early conquests at the hotel had informed one of the hard-core fan sites for Jay's band that his current hideaway was hiring staff. The anonymous "Miss P" had linked the resort's advertisement for cleaning staff, with a note underneath that the only room servicing they'd actually do would involve the rock star himself. They'd hired and fired a dozen girls who couldn't even operate a vacuum cleaner before one of them whined about the job being nothing like she'd signed up for, and she clued them in about the fansite ad. Now they had no cleaning staff for the peak season, even after two rounds of applications, because the housekeeping manager flatly refused to interview anyone else.

She'd then produced a series of increasingly heated emails between Meier and Annette, the housekeeping manager, dating back to when Jay had apparently first purchased the hotel during the peak season the previous year. Around the time of her own arrival in Broome, Xan mused, and when she'd seen the prick for the first time.

The resort was in trouble and Jay was just the turd on the cake. She'd need a plan — two of them, probably. One to keep Jay out of her hair and maybe even get him to leave the island, and one to attract more guests to the hotel. The thought was exhilarating — for the first time, she'd get to properly use her degree and at a place as awesome as

Romance Island. She almost forgave Meier for not straight out telling her about the change of position. Almost.

The signs had all been there. He'd asked interview questions about her experience in supervising and retaining staff; working without supervision…and the kicker was when he'd seemed surprised that all she wanted to discuss about her contract was the probation period. Xan had checked the original emailed contract. Sure enough, it said she was agreeing to be the hotel manager, too. As for her visa documents…Xan grimaced. Her visa was dependent on her retaining her position as the hotel's manager. Any change effectively nullified her visa and put her on the first plane home.

The one place in the world she didn't want to be.

Bugger Jerome and his betrayal. If he hadn't slept with Kelly, hadn't deserted Xan and been too much of a bloody coward to tell her, she would have read everything properly. She wouldn't have missed details like agreeing to run a whole hotel instead of just their tours.

If she told anyone how badly she'd stuffed up, she'd lose any respect the existing staff might have for her. What was an already challenging job would become downright impossible. She'd be damned before she gave up. At least, if she gave up before she found out if there really was a lagoon monster.

Xan laughed. The sound echoed off the tiles and bare walls, but she didn't care. Some time over the last two days, she'd started thinking about the island as hers. Jerome and Kelly and Jay could go to hell for all she cared. She'd just been handed the biggest opportunity of her career, and she was going to make the most of it. Just as long as she didn't mess it up.

That meant getting the lay of the land before she started putting plans in place. Sighing, she switched off her PC and made her way to the staff dining room. The sounds of clinking crockery and muffled laughter reached her before she stepped inside, but it already held a comfy camaraderie she'd never known at the backpackers. These staff had worked together for years, through changes in ownership and now new management. They knew the resort better than she ever could without putting in the same time and dedication, and they all had their own ideas on how the place should be run.

Xan glanced around. Who hadn't she sat with yet? Her eyes landed on a table occupied by two men who obviously worked in IT. It was time she learned about the resort's computer system and the wristbands everyone wore. As it was, Jay knew the ID system better than she did, and that would never do. He might own the hotel, but it was her baby now.

TWENTY-SEVEN

Day three. Xan couldn't wait to get started. She'd woken a dozen times in the night with ideas about how to entice new guests to the resort. Romance Island would blossom under her care.

She breathed in the awakening aroma from her coffee cup and gazed at the piece of paradise framed by her office window. A jetty thrusting out into the aqua-blue sea, while the teasing water licked and kissed the jetty's legs in torturous foreplay as it crept higher until it engulfed the jutting length completely in warm wetness.

Where the hell had that come from?

Xan felt blood rushing to her face. She should have been talking to staff at breakfast, not reading the steamy book Annette from Housekeeping had lent her yesterday. The island infrastructure shouldn't be seeing more action than she was.

A rattling trolley broke the romance of the scene, wheeled by a girl in a maid's uniform. When she reached the end of the jetty — not its head, Xan reminded herself — she lifted a hand to her eyes to scan the water. Xan spotted it the same time as the girl: a boat skimming across the sea surface. She wasn't sure what intrigued her more — her first sight of the speeding carrier boat or the first woman under thirty she'd seen on the island in the week she'd been there.

Down went the coffee and up she got, striding out the building and along the boat dock to where the girl waited.

"Good morning!" Xan called, waving.

The girl responded with a small smile and a chin lift that Xan associated more with guys greeting than girls.

Undeterred, Xan closed the distance between them. "I'm not sure we've met. I'm Xan Lane, the new manager." She held out her hand.

"I'm Pamela, but you don't want to shake my hand right now, Miz Lane." Pamela dropped her gaze to her shoes. "This trolley's full of dirty linen, ready to go to the mainland on the laundry truck. Maybe when I've washed my hands. I saw you in the staff dining room the other night. Mr Meier, he never ate with the rest of us, but I think you're different." She met Xan's eyes once more and laughed a little. "You don't look old enough to be managing a whole hotel."

"I'm probably not," Xan found herself saying. "But I managed Broome Backpackers at Cable Beach and I have a university degree in tourism management, so I am qualified." She sighed. "Meier never told me why he picked me for the job. He just left."

Pamela grinned. "Yeah, Mr Meier didn't like the new

owner, but he's wanted to leave since before that. I often overheard Mr Meier talking to Dennis in security when I was cleaning the foyer. They'd get into one of Mr Meier's bottles of rum and spill all the resort's secrets."

"Like what?"

Pamela just shook her head.

Of course solving the island's mysteries wouldn't be that easy.

"So what do you think of the new owner?" Xan persisted.

More head-shaking. "Jay Felix is a rock star. He owns the hotel, but he doesn't run it. We do. As long as I do my job and get paid for it, it doesn't matter to me who owns the place. This was my people's land long before there was any such thing as a hotel. The lagoon was my uncle's favourite spearfishing spot until his father sold it." Pamela's eyes misted over in keeping with her faraway smile. "I might be just a cleaner here but I'm not stupid, Miz Lane. I'm going to study nursing at Charles Darwin University this year, and I need this job to pay for my books and everything. Living off the land isn't as straightforward as it was before."

Xan couldn't seem to close her mouth. She wasn't sure whether to apologise or agree with her. Fortunately, a shout from the approaching boat ended their conversation as Baz, the skipper, insisted on being introduced.

In the bustle of unloading and loading the boat, Xan found herself alongside Pamela, tossing laundry bags to the deck, while Baz stacked boxes onto the empty trolley.

"These came in on one of the scenic flights yesterday. They've been sitting in town for the last week, waiting for the road to reopen, but the bottle shop got sick of storing it, so they added it to our order. Max can stop complaining about his missing rum now." He hefted one more box onto the trolley. "Hey, if you've replaced him, guess that's yours now, Xan. Don't drink it all at once."

Rum? A whole case of the stuff? Xan hadn't drunk that much rum in her entire life.

"Hey, have you ever been jet boating in a whirlpool, Xan?"

Her heart leaped. Xan forgot about being the responsible manager of anything. "No. Where do I sign up? It sounds awesome." She could always work late, or through her lunch break, to make up the time. And it sort of was work, familiarising herself with the resort's supply lines between the island and the mainland…

Baz jerked his head at the carrier boat. "I got time now. I'm headed back to the farm to meet the truck, but they only reopened the road this morning, so the truck's at least an hour away. The tide's just right, too. Bet you've never seen anything like the Kimberley tides where you're from."

With a deafening clatter, Pamela began pushing the trolley back up the jetty toward the resort.

"In the UK, no, but I managed the backpackers at Cable Beach before I came here." Xan feasted her eyes on the ocean she'd never, ever get enough of. "If more people from home could see this place, they'd never leave. The UK would be empty."

Baz chuckled. "Yeah, most of the British explorers couldn't get enough of this part of the country. Lots of 'em died trying to tame it, too. Can't tame the Kimberley." He shoved the last two laundry bags in a storage locker and slammed it shut. "Grab a seat in the bow. You'll want to hang on when we get to Pearl Passage. It's a wild ride with the tide coming in."

Xan climbed aboard and straddled one of the seats at the front of the boat, glad she'd chosen to wear pants today. The boat was basically a giant inflatable with a carpeted deck. And cushy foam rollercoaster seats.

Baz cast off and eased the boat away from the jetty until it pointed at the distant mainland. "Hold on!" he shouted as the engine's contented purr rose into a challenging roar. For a moment, they skimmed across the surface of the water, mounting a cresting wave before flying over the top to bump into the trough between it and the next. A spume of spray soaked Xan to the skin, but she just laughed as she rode the best rollercoaster she'd ever seen. Wind plastered her shirt to her chest. She was doubly glad she'd braided her hair today or she'd look like she wore a seaweed wig when she returned to her office. Ah, what would it matter? She'd need to shower off the salt, anyway. But later. Later, because right now she intended to just enjoy the moment, zipping across the water like a flying fish as the rust and cream layered cliffs grew closer.

The boat slowed, idling like the world's biggest aquatic motorcycle, and Baz bellowed, "The farm just radioed to say they need me to head straight back. You okay to come with me? You won't be stuck on the mainland for more than an hour or so, when I do the next island supply run, or I can get Shou to run you back in the helicopter."

"It's fine!" she shouted back. She might as well see the facilities on the mainland and meet the rest of the staff at the pearl farm. Her plans for the resort would involve them, too.

"We're going into King Sound now, and the tide's coming in, so it's going to get a bit rough. You'll need to hold on until we get through the whirlpools. They're pretty unpredictable. I'll do my best to get you close without going in, but that means turning suddenly. You ready?"

Xan pried one white-knuckled hand off the bar to signal a diver's okay in the air above her head. Even if she wasn't, there was no way on Earth she'd back down now. Hell, she wanted to get behind the wheel of this baby herself, though it was probably safest that she didn't. She was a dive master, not a boat master. If ever an experience made her want to change that…

Baz rounded the cliffs and the boat accelerated, carried by the racing tide. He swerved and sent the boat careening around the edge of a spectacular vortex before the surface smoothed like a placid lake, only for turbulence to swirl another into being directly ahead of them. Xan tipped sideways, holding on for dear life, as Baz dodged around rocks and whirlpools, whooping at the top of his lungs.

Not that Xan was any quieter, but she cherished the hope that Baz would be a gentleman about it and not tell the resort staff that she was a screamer. Who needed sex when adrenaline-pumping whirlpool surfing was part of your normal work day?

The warmth of the sun heated her skin as the demanding wind caressed her body through her clothes. The bass rumble of the engine thrummed until her bones vibrated right along with it, the sheer power of all of it fighting with the mighty ocean for control over her body, thrusting her deep into her seat like an impatient lover who would not be denied. She felt like she'd swallowed a case of champagne, but the taste of salt on her lips told her otherwise. No sex was this good.

Xan sat back, laughing quietly to herself. She felt the boat slow, but the steamy humidity that settled on her as they approached the farm didn't make it easy for her to catch her breath. She fanned her face, hoping Baz didn't notice, but as he pulled up in the shallows Xan found him at her side, offering a hand to help her off the boat. She accepted his assistance, staggering to her feet on rubbery legs that felt like she'd run…no, engaged in a marathon of a very different sort.

"Was it as good for you as it was for me?" Baz asked.

Xan couldn't wipe the grin off her face as she replied, "Oh no, it was better."

She burst out laughing when Baz blushed bright red.

They parted on a pretty lawn beside the pool, with Baz promising to come get her when it was time to leave again. In the meantime, maybe she'd like to grab a drink in the restaurant upstairs?

The pearl farm restaurant wasn't open yet, but the manager offered to make Xan a coffee anyway, which she gratefully accepted. Ambrosia – especially after leaving her first coffee back on her desk at the resort. The thrilling ride had been worth it, plus she still had the trip home to look forward to. Xan hoped she'd have the stamina for a second round on the jet boat.

She glanced at the TV in the corner, recognising one of the morning shows that was equal parts news and sales pitch for whatever products paid to advertise with them. Today's news was about the stupid but tragic things tourists did when they didn't understand the harsh environment out here. A couple of backpackers' bodies had been found, drowned in a flooded river south of Hedland. The frowning news anchor said they were still looking for a third tourist whose body hadn't yet been found, though she was seen travelling with the other two.

Xan shook her head. She didn't want to hear any more. Too many tourists took risks that cost them their lives. Driving onto a flooded road was more dangerous than you realised, if you didn't know how deep it was. She didn't want to see the faces of this bunch of unfortunates – what if they were guests she'd met at the Broome Backpackers?

Nodding her thanks to the manager, she left the restaurant and perched on a rock beside the horizon pool. She wanted to get back to Romance Island. There was so much to do.

As if he'd read her mind, Baz appeared at the top of the steps. To be fair, just his head appeared, huffing and puffing, then his torso, several thumping steps later, followed by the rest of him, half leaning on the handrail and thoroughly out of breath. He took his time recovering before he said, "Right. Next time I'm going to shout at you from the boat ramp below. We're just loading the boat up now. Should be fifteen, maybe twenty minutes, and we'll be on our way back. And…I've got a passenger. New staff member headed out to the hotel for the first time. Her car broke down on the road a ways back, so she didn't arrive until this morning in the laundry truck. Come and I'll introduce you." He waved her over and started down the steps again.

New staff? She hadn't approved any new staff.

Something smelled fishy and it wasn't the farm's oysters. Xan strode after Baz, expecting trouble. She wouldn't be disappointed.

TWENTY-EIGHT

IT'S BEEN DAYS, BABY. WHY WON'T YOU TALK
TO ME?

Days. How many days? Too many. He'd sent message after message, full of frogs and mermaids and other half-remembered fairy tale stuff, but Phuong hadn't responded. He'd scared her off by talking about knights and proposals, but he'd expected one of her sassy comebacks, not silence. Silence for fucking days. What'd he done wrong?

Not drunk enough bourbon, that's what. Pity there was none left. He'd have to visit the bar and liberate some more.

Maybe there was something in those romance books that he'd missed. After all, they were basically adult fairy tales, ending happily ever after with awesome sex. Everything should end with awesome sex. And start with it, too.

Jay hoisted himself off the couch and padded outside.

His bare feet made almost no sound on the sand as he avoided the well-lit public pathways by taking the secret jungle tracks he'd made in his time on the island. This one was the most well-worn, probably because it led to his two favourite places – the library and the pub.

Not that he wanted to keep his visits to the pub secret. His trips to the library, however…what would people say if they saw him with an armload of romance books? Nobody would believe that he was trying to research the fuck out of the things.

Because being a rock star wasn't enough.

He knew that now. Now that he wasn't one any more, not really. He figured he still had rock god status, but he wasn't a star any more if he didn't perform.

That's why he'd gone for a girl with a foreign-sounding name who was looking for a fairy tale, because he figured he could deliver on that bit if he just read enough of the right books. He'd read them again and again, the ones on mail-order brides. Until he knew what he'd done wrong. He'd send another message, the perfect one that made everything all right again, and she'd come to the island and they'd live happily ever after and shit.

Yeah.

He rounded the last palm tree, edging carefully past the spiky pandanus, before emerging behind Meier's house. No, not any more. Meier had left, hadn't he? There was a new manager. The bitch with the bucket, who'd tried to drown him the other day.

Jason glanced at the veranda and grinned. The stacked boxes of supplies by her front door gave him a brilliant idea for revenge. Meier had always ordered a case of rum with his food order and there it was, right on top. He just felt like a drink, too.

He ripped into the box and grabbed two bottles of rum. Tucking them under his arms, he whistled as he walked through the deserted staff dongas to the library. It wasn't open to guests yet, but that wouldn't stop him. His ID was a skeleton key, allowing him entry to everywhere at the resort. One swipe and the library door slid open to welcome him inside.

The door hissed shut behind him and not a moment too soon – he heard male voices and approaching footsteps. Good thing he knew the resort's security system so well. Tapping his wristband, Jay set a 'do not disturb' sign on the library door, effectively locking it against everyone else at the resort. Now he could read in peace.

Grabbing a book in one hand and a bottle in the other, he unscrewed the cap and took a swig. Fuck yeah. This was the life. Reading with rum. By the end of the day, he'd charm Phuong's pants off. Just like Americans in books did to their mail-order brides…

TWENTY-NINE

"So what brings you to Romance Island?"

Phuong jerked awake, looking around for the source of the question. She sat up and spotted the woman who'd spoken, though she didn't look much older than herself. She looked a whole lot neater, though.

Phuong glanced down at her own clothes, so covered in the road's red dust from walking on it last night that even she couldn't tell what colour they'd been originally. She wanted a shower and a lot of sleep, but she couldn't rest until she was safe on the island with Jason.

"I…I'm sorry?" Phuong mumbled.

The woman repeated her question.

"Oh. I'm here for Jason. He told me to come."

Suspicion narrowed the woman's eyes. "Jason? So you're a big fan of his, I take it?"

How could she possibly explain to this stranger that

she'd fallen head over heels in love with a man she knew better than she knew herself, but she'd never met? It sounded crazy even to her. "More than that. We're going to be married." Phuong thanked the dust caking her skin for covering her blush before she got her cheeks under control.

Suspicion hardened to disbelief. "Married? Well, good luck with that."

Tears sprang to Phuong's eyes. Did she doubt him? Had she driven all this way, through raging rivers and roads that stretched endlessly to the horizon, only to be disappointed in Jason, too? Jason would take care of her, she was certain of it. "I might not look like much, but I've driven all the way from Perth to see him. My car broke down on the dirt road and I walked, walked all night, until a truck picked me up and brought me here. They said there's a boat to the island. He's there. He said he would be. Jason's the sweetest, kindest, most charming man I've ever met, anywhere, and he'll marry me, just like he said."

"He let you drive here, all this way, by yourself?"

"He didn't know," Phuong whispered. "I wanted to surprise him."

"I see." Judging by the woman's tone, she saw things that made her very thoughtful, but she didn't say any more.

Phuong was too tired to care. So close to her final destination. The Englishwoman could keep her secrets if she just let her sleep a little longer...

"So, getting along well, ladies?"

Phuong had barely closed her eyes before the sun-baked man was back. She struggled to rise again.

"We're done loading. First and final boarding call for the *Argo* travelling to Romance Island Resort. All aboard!"

The Englishwoman climbed confidently into a seat at the front of the boat, but Phuong didn't feel that brave. She wasn't sure she'd trust any body of water for a long time yet. She huddled in a seat at the very back, partially sheltered under the canopy that housed the console where the skipper stood, and hugged her dusty bag to her chest.

"The tide's almost in, so it'll be a calm trip today, ladies. Not like this morning, eh, Xan?"

The woman in the front seat – Xan – laughed. "Next time, Baz. I'm hooked."

"What about you, Phuong? D'you like thrilling rides?" Baz persisted.

Phuong shook her head. She'd never been fond of Universal Studios or the waterslides back home. Rough rides and rollercoasters just weren't her thing at all. "I just want to get to the island in one piece," she said.

"You will, sweetheart. We've never lost anyone overboard and we won't today. Keep an eye out for dolphins – I saw a pod this morning on my way out, but haven't seen them since. They're around, though."

Phuong didn't respond. She was too busy fighting her rising panic as the boat took off like a car racing away from the traffic lights, pressing her back into her seat. It was sort of smooth at first, and she loosened her grip on the shiny metal bar beside her seat. She dared to glance up at the sea.

Instead of the pale aqua surrounding the boat when she'd boarded, now the ocean stretched out in ripples of sapphire edged in white lace, all the way to the horizon. Waves...open water...and a grey fin slicing through the water. Sharks? The ocean was worse than any of the swollen rivers she'd struggled through to get here.

Just let her make it to the island alive, she prayed. Not drowned or eaten by a shark or anything else...

The boat flew up a wave and bumped into the bit in between. Her stomach swooped, promising she'd be sick if she'd stopped to eat anything before boarding the boat. The boat bumped again, harder this time, and a whimper escaped from her throat, one she hoped no one heard.

Squeezing her eyes shut, Phuong hung on and hoped. What more could she do? Jason waited for her at the end of this torturous trip, while behind was Norman.

Her stomach roiled as the boat rose and fell with the waves, speeding ever onwards. Phuong lost count of the number of times her teeth clacked together as the boat landed hard on water that felt as hard as rock. One thing was certain: she never wanted to set foot on a boat again.

When she'd endured all the bumping she could take, the boat arced into a turn, throwing her against the side of her seat, before it shuddered to a stop. Phuong dared to open her eyes.

The boat bobbed beside a wooden jetty that blocked her view of anything else. Baz began passing plastic-wrapped packages up to someone up top while Xan scaled the ladder and stepped out of sight.

"We're here. Welcome to Romance Island Resort," Baz said, reaching for Phuong's bag.

She surrendered it and watched it float out of sight as unseen hands lifted it onto the jetty.

"Your turn." Baz jerked his head at the ladder.

Phuong rose and grabbed the handrail. Her rubbery legs threatened to fold up beneath her. Six shaky steps took her to the edge of the boat. The first rung of the ladder felt warm to the touch. Her shoe slipped as she set her foot on one of the lower rungs, but she just tightened her fingers around the dry ones higher up until she regained her footing. Anything was better than the boat, she promised herself, as she hauled her exhausted body onto dry land.

When both her feet stood firmly on the jetty timbers, Phuong dared to look up. What she saw dropped her to her knees.

Paradise. Finally, she was home.

THIRTY

Bloody hell. She might be a crazed fangirl, but that didn't mean she didn't deserve help. Xan didn't doubt the girl's story for a minute, though she'd filled in the gaps with her own assumptions. Between the reddened eyes, shaky legs that barely held the girl's slight weight, and dust-caked clothes, she'd travelled a long way through trying conditions to get here. How that dickhead could inspire such devotion, she had no idea. Poor, pitiful… What was her name again? Fong?

Xan offered the girl her hand and helped her to her feet.

"The resort's this way. I'll speak to Reception and arrange a room for you."

The girl's gaze dropped to her shoes. "It's all right. I can't…I don't…it doesn't matter." She swallowed. "Can I just see Jason?" There was a quiet desperation in her tone that squeezed Xan's heart.

"Don't you want to freshen up first? Look your best and all? You won't be charged for the room." Xan hid her crossed fingers behind her back. The half-formed plan she'd devised on the boat depended on the girl holding Jay's attention long enough to distract him from both the staff and the way Xan ran the hotel. Half-dead and covered in a layer of dust so thick it had formed a sort of crust over her skin as it dried, Jay wouldn't look twice at her. She'd charge the room to Jay – it's not like he'd notice.

The girl wavered. Xan smelled victory.

"All right."

Xan kept pace with the girl's stumbling strides until they reached Reception.

Toby visibly sagged in relief. "Ms Lane, I've been trying to reach you for the last hour. There's a situation that needs your attention in the library…" He stopped abruptly when he caught sight of the girl.

"Her car broke down on the Cape Leveque Road. Can you take her to a hotel room, please? And locate the owner. In the meantime, I'll take care of the library."

Toby nodded smartly. "Yes, ma'am. If you'll put this on, miss, and follow me." He handed the girl a slim wristband that looked nothing like the bulky device on Xan's wrist.

Xan waited for them to leave the foyer before she marched to the library. One of the IT guys – Cam? She'd have to go through the personnel files again and memorise those names, damn it – knelt by the door scanner, jabbing his finger at a tablet tethered to the scanner.

"Fucking open!" he growled at the door. He resumed poking the tablet.

"What's the problem with the library? Please tell me it's

not Professor Plum with the candlestick standing over a dead body in there." At Xan's blank look, she added, "Cluedo? The board game?" She gave up waiting for recognition. "What's the problem?"

"Annette from Housekeeping reported this morning that the door's locked. No one can get in, not even staff. The computer says someone's tripped the privacy lock on it, but that's not possible. Only guests can do that to their rooms. Staff can lock public areas, of course, but that comes up as a fault, not 'do not disturb'. And it won't tell me who the ID's allocated to. Just gives me a damn number!" He bared his teeth and actually growled.

Xan wanted to laugh, but she had better things to do than listen to a tech guy's rambling. "So what do you expect me to do?"

He stared at her, wide-eyed. "You're the manager, the only one who can override it."

"Right." Xan lifted her wrist to the scanner and her wristband emitted a high-pitched beep. She peered at the display. "Will you look at that? It says the door's locked."

"You have to hold it for longer."

Xan leaned against the wall, her patience rapidly draining away. "How much longer?"

A series of beeps chirped from the scanner before Xan's wristband flashed, asking her if she wanted to override the door lock. About bloody time. She tapped the screen and it went blank.

"If that worked, then I should be able to – " Cam swiped his ID and the door hissed open. He sagged against the wall.

An unholy stench rolled out of the library. Xan almost

gagged. "Go check the guest register for Professor Plum," she managed to say before she pinched her nose shut. She should at least get a glimpse of the body before she called the police.

There wasn't much blood, she noticed with some relief as she sidled into the room. The god-awful smell intensified, but she pushed on. The bookshelves looked pretty clean. Presumably that meant the body had been hidden pretty well, as it wasn't visible to anyone entering the room or walking past.

Xan edged around the sofa before she spotted the corpse, sprawled out on the floor in the narrow gap between the sofa and the bookshelf behind it. The body twitched. Xan leaped back, swearing.

"Fuck, pipe down," the body said, rolling over to squint at her. "How'd you get in here?" Jay knocked over a glass bottle, sending it spinning across the floor.

"It doesn't matter. This is the guests' library. What are you doing here?" she demanded.

Jay studied the shelves. "Looking for a good thriller. Lots of sex and swearing and shit. You know."

"In the erotica section," Xan said flatly. Now she really wanted to laugh. The resort's Don Juan having to read up on sex? No, she didn't believe it.

"Huh?" He didn't deny it – he just shrugged. "Gets boring without any company. No good-looking chicks on this island." A malevolent glare dared her to argue.

Xan allowed herself a tiny smile. "Oh, but that's just not true. Your friend Fong arrived this morning."

His eyes widened. "Phuong? She's here? Oh, thank fuck. Where is she?" He leaped to his feet, which might have been more impressive, if he didn't immediately slip over on the source of the stench. He scrambled up again. "Fuck. I need a shower." He grabbed a stack of books on the sofa, shoved past Xan and left. Sadly, the smell didn't go with him.

"Oh, good, you got it open." Annette strode into the room, before she noticed the mess. Her face fell. "He was in the library? What was he doing here?"

Xan surveyed the floor. "Well, it looks like he drank himself into a stupor, threw it all up over the floor and the bottom shelf of the BDSM section, then borrowed a bunch of books and decided to go home." She pointed at the vomit-covered books. "What do we do with those? Can they be cleaned?"

Annette glanced at the shelf. "We'll just throw them out. No one will miss them."

Xan bridled at the insult to readers and authors of erotica everywhere. "Now, hang on. I happen to know a lot of people read those books. The backpackers I worked at only had a tiny library, but those titles were the most read books we had. Surely there's something we can do to clean them."

To Xan's surprise, Annette laughed. "Honey, that shelf's full of spare copies of the *Fifty Shades* books. We have boxes of them in the store room and four shelves full of them in this room alone. Believe me, no one will miss a couple dozen spares." She winked. "And if you're after her new one, I'm almost finished with my copy. I can loan it to you after I'm done."

Xan didn't know where to look. "All right then."

Annette nodded. "I'll get a cleaning crew in here to sort

this out so we can open the library for guests again. Hey, where are all those gone?" She pointed at an empty shelf bearing the sign: MILITARY ROMANCE.

"Jay Felix just left with an armful of books. You don't think…"

"God no!"

They both laughed. A rock star who read romance books? Never happen.

THIRTY-ONE

Phuong stood under the shower spray until her road-dust body paint was nothing more than a small, muddy drift on the floor tiles, headed down the drain. It had taken her most of the complimentary shower gel and soap, but she figured that's what the hotel put them there for. She still wasn't sure she'd managed to shampoo all the sand out of her hair, but maybe she could brush it out when it dried. Reluctantly, she shut off the water and reached for a towel. Even the white flannel was its own brand of bliss – soft and thick, it enveloped her like a lover's arms. The sort who only wanted to cuddle and never, ever demanded sex like it was his right.

No, don't think about that now, she told herself. Things would be different with Jason.

Phuong looked longingly at the bed, wishing she could sleep for a week, but she didn't belong in this luxurious hotel room. She belonged with Jason. She had to find him so she could answer his proposal. How could she say anything but yes?

The phone on the nightstand purred, pulling out of her reverie. "Hello?"

"Is this Ph…Phu-ong?"

"Yes."

"I have a message for you. From…Jason. He says he'll be waiting for you at Villa Penguin, which is the last house on the path on the other side of the lagoon from the hotel. Awaiting your pleasure, when you're ready." The receptionist coughed. "Do you have a response for him?"

Phuong's heart sang. "Yes. Tell him I'll be right down. As soon as I get changed. Right down." She ended the call and crossed the room to her bag. Thankfully, she hadn't gotten much dust into it, so her crumpled clothes were mostly unharmed. She dug out a dress she'd worn a million times in her fantasies about their first meeting, but still had the tags on it from the shop where she'd bought it in Singapore. She'd planned on wearing it for Chinese New Year, but Norman had scoffed at the thought of celebrating something so stupid, so she'd put it away instead of arguing. Funny. She'd started the new year without him, but now would be the perfect time to wear her celebration dress as she stepped into a future with good fortune instead of bad.

She brushed her hair, pinned it up, then let it down again, not sure what do. In the end, she brushed it back into a ponytail. Her hands shook as she applied her makeup, so she kept it minimal for fear of making a mistake. It wouldn't do to show up with panda eyes and so much lipstick that he wouldn't kiss her.

Would he be a good kisser?

Her cheeks reddened, forcing her to drop the blush back into her makeup bag. No, she didn't need any more colour. This would be enough. It wouldn't do to keep Jason waiting.

Phuong buckled on her favourite heels, hoping to enhance her height by an extra couple of inches to place her lips within easy reach. She didn't want him to hesitate. Or, worse, reject her.

Hair down. Definitely down. She ripped out the ponytail holder and left it on the counter.

So much rested on their first meeting.

Please don't let me stuff this up! Phuong begged the universe, knowing it didn't care, but hoping luck would run her way for once. Just this once…

Phuong forced herself to step out of the hotel room and made her way down to the foyer to ask for directions to Villa Penguin. The receptionist pointed to the path outside, insisting that it was impossible to miss – all she had to do was follow the path around the lagoon until it ended at the last villa.

She nodded and thanked him. All too soon, she found herself on the butter-coloured paving that led to her destiny.

Straightening her shoulders, she set off. One step after the other, on legs that threatened to give out under her in sheer exhaustion, but determination drove her on. She glimpsed aquamarine waters between the trees, until the path opened up a little and ran beside a tiny, white sand beach. On the other side, an ornate sign informed her that she'd reached the Pearl Villas. Her heart beat faster – she was close.

Phuong read the sign on the first house: VILLA MAXIMA. Then Villas Pinctada, Albina and Margaritifera, making her wonder how many more she'd have to walk past to reach her destination. Oh, how about this next one? No, it was Villa Akoya. Phuong never thought she'd be sick of pearls, but right now, all she wanted was a penguin.

The path ended abruptly in a patch of red dust that reminded her of last night's tortuous trek. Another, narrower path led off between the palm trees bearing the welcome message: VILLA PENGUIN.

Phuong's breath caught in her throat. Here it was. Jason's house. Just through those trees…

She had to force herself to breathe – deeply in, out, in, out several times before she could take another step. What if he didn't like her?

What if he decided she wasn't worth his time because she'd taken so long to get here?

Fear pushed her forward when nothing else did. She had to see him.

The villa overlooked the ocean. It even had its own private jetty, a copy of the loading dock on the other side of the island. And a front door, which now stood only inches in front of her. Close enough to reach out and touch, or knock on to announce her arrival.

Nervousness overwhelmed Phuong. What-ifs swirled through her head and made her lightheaded. Tears welled up, threatening to spill. She couldn't cry until after she'd met him, or her scant makeup would wash off. She had to be brave or all was lost.

Lifting her strangely numb hand, she touched her

knuckles to the glass. No sound. She took a deep breath and rapped smartly on the frosted glass door.

"Knock, knock, who's there?" called a deep voice that made her stomach churn. She hadn't counted on him having a sexy voice to go with the ripped body. It sounded better than she'd imagined.

"It's Phuong," she squeaked, then cursed herself and repeated her name, desperately trying to sound less like a cartoon character, but she wasn't sure if she succeeded.

"Ah, the mysterious Phuong," came the voice from the other side of the door, where she could see a hulking shadow. The man was huge – surely he couldn't really be that big. A trick of the light, maybe. The door whooshed open.

Phuong found herself face to face with the man who featured in her wildest fantasies. His laughing eyes were the colour of honey. The dark, red-brown honey from flowering gum trees that cost way more than the sugary, cheap stuff they'd served in the college dining room. The sort promising sweetness but also so much more. The eyes of the man she'd crossed the state for, welcoming her home.

"Jay Felix, your very own frog, at your service." He gestured down the length of his body before he held out his arms. "Now, how about that kiss?"

Phuong looked. Arms strong enough to hold her, to protect her from anything.

And looked. The abs were real, so real she could reach out and touch them.

And looked again. The treasure trail was real, too, guiding her eyes down to…

The only sound that came out of her throat was the squeak of a dying mouse. No, not a dying mouse. One faced with an enormous snake. But she liked living.

She opened her mouth and released a second squeak.

So she did the only thing that made sense at the time: she bolted.

THIRTY-TWO

She wasn't eavesdropping. Not even a little bit. Just because she'd accidentally overheard Toby talking to Jay and then decided to stretch her legs in the corridor behind Reception as Toby conveyed Jay's message to Phuong, requesting a meeting at Villa Penguin, wherever that was...no, it still wasn't eavesdropping. Where was Villa Penguin, anyway? Presumably near the jetty named after the same bird.

Xan hadn't been hiding behind the potted palms, waiting for Phuong to appear. They'd just sort of screened her from sight, like they were supposed to screen the whole service corridor. She'd only moved them a little bit. Hardly at all. So when Phuong finally appeared in an elegant red dress with matching heels, of course Xan had felt the need to go outside for some air.

The best scenic path led around the lagoon to the Pearl Villas, so it was only natural that she'd choose to walk that way. It had nothing to do with the clacking red shoes she could hear just around the bend. She'd just passed Villa Pinctada when she heard a voice calling her name.

Damn the man.

"Ms Lane," huffed Lee the maintenance man. "Just need to inform you about the shark. Seems we've got a tiger shark in the lagoon. It's just within the legal size for fishing. A few more inches and he'd be too big. The chefs want it caught so they can serve fresh shark fin soup, but the occupational health and safety manager insists it should be chased out of the lagoon at the next high tide. What do you want me to do?"

Xan stared blankly at him for a moment. Since when did her job include deciding the fate of sharks?

Since she became the manager of this living aquarium, she reminded herself.

"What did you do to the last tiger shark that got into the lagoon?"

Lee grinned. "Fish and chips in the staff dining room."

Xan felt sick. She had no problems swimming with sharks, but when it came to catching them… "Do you have all the gear you need to catch it?"

"Sure do, Ms Lane. There'll be fresh fish for lunch tomorrow, you'll see."

She swallowed, nodded and walked away, hurrying in her hope of catching up to Phuong in time to witness the fangirl's first meeting with the dickhead of her dreams.

Xan could just read the sign on Villa Akoya when she heard the slap of running feet. No, not just running; fleeing in terror, judging by Phuong's expression. The girl didn't even see her. She just kept running until she vanished around the bend. Xan called after her, but received no response.

Now, should she follow the girl and make sure she was okay, or find out what had frightened her? Maybe she'd seen the tiger shark. Phuong had looked terrified on the boat ride over, even though the Sound had been flat as a millpond the whole way. Ooh, what if she'd seen the sea monster? Xan wouldn't give up a chance at seeing if there really was one.

There. Decision made.

Xan strode confidently forward until she found…a shoe. One of Phuong's shiny, red heels, lying on the path that led to the Penguin jetty. Xan sighed, picked it up, and headed for the jetty. Around the next bend, she found the second shoe. Now she had a matching pair, though they were far too tiny for her size nine feet. Well-loved, too, judging by how worn the soles were. Hardly something a girl would leave behind unless she was running for her life. But from what? No sharks or sea monsters at the villa. Just…Jay.

Xan marched up the veranda and pounded on his door, making it shake in its frame. "Jay Felix, what did you do to that girl?"

Silence.

"If you did anything to harm her, don't think I won't call the police! I know every officer in the station. No amount of money will make this go away. I'll make sure of it!" she continued, pounding on the door some more.

"Fuck off. I didn't touch her. She just ran away," Jay shouted from inside.

"She was terrified. I saw her face. You must have been a

right bastard to make Cinderella forget her favourite shoes!" Xan waved the footwear, hoping he could see the heels through the frosted glass.

The door hissed open and Xan pulled her hand back before she knocked on his chest. "Yeah? You think I'm a bastard for offering her everything? For letting her know exactly what she's getting when she marries me?" He ripped the shoes out of her hands. "You go manage my hotel, Xan. Stay out of my love life. That's way above your pay grade."

"You answered the door like that?" Xan waved at his body, but her eyes were stuck on his midsection. One particular part of his midsection, standing to attention and saluting her, for God's sake. He looked like a Greek statue come to life. A naked statue, and she'd honestly thought no man could really look like that. The ancients had used plenty of artistic licence, she'd been certain, but the man in front of her put paid to all that.

His voice turned dark and sexy. "Yes, I did. Like I said, I offered her everything and gave her a good look at the goods. What's wrong, Xan? Jealous?"

No. Appalled that such a waste of space was allowed such a gorgeous body.

Xan raised her head and looked him in the eye. No, not that eye…the ones on his face. "Jay," she said coolly, "Put some damn pants on, will you? No wonder that girl fled like the devil was after her. You're a bloody wanker. I hope she calls the papers when she gets back to her room and tells them every damn detail."

She turned her back on the rock star and marched back to her office.

So much for distracting Jay with female company. A

media shit-storm would have to do; one that kept Jay on the mainland for a long time.

As she walked, she wondered: what would she have done in Phuong's place, faced with her idol in all his naked glory? Xan wouldn't have run. She'd have taken what she wanted and…and…

Lost it, just like Jerome.

Bugger. Bugger, bugger, double-bloody-buggered bastard.

Xan's shoulders slumped. Her pace slowed until she was almost dragging her feet back to the office. The office, that's right. She had work to do. Planning for the future of this paradise.

Now she'd found the snake. A sizeable one, to be sure, but it was firmly attached to the hotel's owner. It wouldn't be escaping to bother her again any time soon, Xan swore.

THIRTY-THREE

By the time she'd run out of breath, Phuong already regretted running, and she couldn't even see the main hotel building yet. He'd asked for a kiss. Just a kiss. She should have just given it to him. Instead, she'd ruined everything.

Jason wasn't Norman; the two men were worlds apart. Jason had a body even she admitted she admired; a sexy voice she hadn't expected and…it had to be a joke, surely. Candid cameras must have captured her shocked reaction when she discovered the man who wanted her to be his mail-order bride was none other than Jay Felix, Chaya frontman and hot rock star. All the things he'd said in his messages fell into place. Wanting more than just one-night stands and holiday romances; needing something more. Even she knew the man's reputation, though she wasn't a huge fan of the band. She probably had one of their albums at home somewhere.

How could she have been so stupid? Men with six-packs didn't need online dating sites to find a bride. Her escape from Norman, the nightmarish road trip, all of it was because of a prank for some reality TV show that would show her as the fool she was, because she'd been desperate enough to believe that she could have a future where fairy tales did come true.

Tears blurred her vision by the time she shoved through the foyer doors. Desperate to reach her room before a single salty droplet fell, she broke into a run again, before she was forced to halt in front of her hotel room door. Where was her key?

She reached for the scanner pad, which beeped. A moment later, the door hissed open. She stumbled through the portal to…oblivion, she hoped. Didn't really care any more.

Running footsteps in the corridor outside stopped just as the door slid shut. "Miss, are you all right? Do you need assistance?"

Phuong rested her head against the cool glass as the dam burst, gushing tears down her face. No. She was a stupid, gullible idiot for falling in love with a fantasy. The only way anyone could help her was by ripping out her traitorous brain and heart, then replacing them with new ones that worked properly.

"Miss, I'll get the manager."

She mumbled something about being fine, though she was anything but fine right now.

Footsteps squeaked away.

Before she could exhale in relief, the phone rang. Should she answer it?

No. She didn't want to see or speak to anyone. She just wanted to sleep and forget all this had ever happened.

Was there a way to lock the door?

Yes, there was. A tiny sign where the doorknob should be said to tap her wristband three times, then hold it beside the scanner until the screen told her the lock was activated. Her arm felt like it was weighted with lead as she lifted it to the scanner that was surely not made with short people in mind. The moment stretched forever before text flashed up on the screen:

DO NOT DISTURB. ENJOY YOUR EVENING.

She wouldn't.

Dragging off her dress, Phuong crawled into bed and surrendered, sobbing, to sleep.

THIRTY-FOUR

He didn't need pants. He needed his phone. He needed to talk to her, to hear that soft voice again. Better than he'd imagined. Prettier than he'd imagined. He needed to find out how he'd fucked up because he was certain he'd done everything right.

That's how it happened in books. All the books. They'd meet online, message and stuff, then meet in person so his irresistible body could seal the deal. Wham, bam, marry me, ma'am and they lived happily ever after.

He'd thought about pants, but he knew he was just as hot below the waist as he was above it, so of course he hadn't worn them. He looked stupid in just a shirt, plus it hid his abs, so a shirt was absolutely out.

Underwear. Maybe he should've worn underwear.

Or was it because he hadn't been wearing thongs, when that's what she'd asked for? Fuck, how could he have forgotten? His and hers, for walking on the beach.

Now he had her shoes, but not the damn girl.

He punched the number for Reception and demanded to be put through to her room. The phone rang and rang, but no one answered.

Was she in her room? Not there yet? On the boat back to the mainland? On a helicopter headed home? Fuck, he didn't even know where she lived. If she left the island, he might never find her again.

Jason slammed the phone back in the cradle. He dialled Reception again.

"Did she leave on the carrier boat? Have there been any helicopter flights this afternoon?" he demanded.

"She arrived on the last carrier boat of the day, and no, Mr Felix, there are no flights scheduled today."

He demanded to know her room number so he could dial direct.

The phone rang until it rang out, so he dialled again. And again.

This was not fucking happening to him.

He called Reception and demanded that they track down her ID.

"Yes, sir. Initiating a search now…" Several very long seconds passed. "She's still on the island, in — "

The phone in Jason's hand let out a warning beep as its battery gave up the ghost. He threw it, not caring where it landed.

He'd have to fucking find her himself, then.

Jason snatched up the shoes and strode out into the sunset. Cinderella was getting her fucking fairy tale ending if it was the last thing he did.

THIRTY-FIVE

Norman was chasing her. He'd never stop, never give up, until he caught her and drained her dry. Relentlessly pursuing her across land and sea and rivers that weren't sure which they were, and tried to make up for it by being extra fierce and sweeping away everything in their path. They wouldn't stop him, though. She'd barely made it across, but he stood on the other side of the torrent, laughing and urging it on as the water licked at her, snapped at her with sharks' teeth and tried to drag her back to his suffocating embrace.

Norman just stood there, sporting fangs of his own, and shouted that she'd die for daring to disobey him.

His voice grew fainter as she turned her back on him. Now, she faced the future. A man whose face she couldn't see. But as she kept running, his features came into focus in the blazing daylight that surrounded him. Jason. Hope had kept her going all this time because she knew if she just reached him, she'd be safe. It didn't matter that he wasn't wearing a scrap of clothing. Where he stood was safe. His arms opened, and she dove into them. Home.

Norman couldn't reach her here. No one could. Norman didn't have fangs – just big, crooked teeth that had made her think of a horse the first time she'd seen him. Now she knew him better, she thought he resembled an ass more than a horse. And a gelded one, at that. But Jason was real, down to the last detail from their meeting yesterday. From his sculpted six-pack right down to his jutting…

And just like that, Phuong surfaced from sleep, blinking against the glare of day blaring its presence through the blinds she'd forgotten to shut.

The previous day's events came flooding back in, all shouting to be heard at once. Walking that endless road, then crossing the ocean and coming face to face with an impossible dream. A naked rock star who couldn't possibly be Jason. But he was.

She wanted to confront him and ask why he'd played such a horrible prank on her. Toying with her feelings and inviting her to his island, when there was no way he'd follow through with his offer. But what good would it do? Knowing why wouldn't change anything. She couldn't live a dream any more.

What could she do now? She had nothing. No car, no money, and just the clothes in her bag. A partially completed business degree and her old school laptop. Maybe she'd ask if the hotel had a job opening – after all, Baz, the ferryman, had thought she was a new employee when he offered to take her to the island. Only for a few weeks, though, when her visa ran out and the new semester started. The one she couldn't afford to attend.

No, that wouldn't work. No business wanted new staff for just a few weeks, only to lose them the moment they were trained. Hardly a good business proposition.

She could go home to Thuan and the rest of her family, what was left of it, and try to find work in Singapore. Like she had any idea where to look.

Her head hurt, and not just from crying half the night, either. Maybe she should find some coffee. After that, she'd take a walk on the beach to clear her head. There had to be something she could do. No way was she going anywhere near the online dating site where she'd met both Norman and Jason. Someone would try to track her, and that would be it. Norman would know how to catch her again.

Coffee, beach, then bigger problems, she promised herself.

Phuong washed and dressed, surprised to find that her reflection looked more human than it had yesterday. No red zombie eyes, at least. No makeup, either, she decided. Not when she wore a t-shirt and shorts and tied her hair back.

Deep breath, then open the door and search for coffee.

Phuong exhaled as the door hissed open. She stepped out into the corridor.

Of course, no amount of meditative breathing could have prepared her for the body lying across her door, where normal people had doormats, or how she tripped on it and landed in a graceless heap on the floor.

"Guess I deserved that, but can you tell me why?" a pained voice said.

Phuong rose slowly, staring at the body curled up like a

cooked prawn. "Who are you, and why were you lying in wait outside my door?" She looked askance at the potted palm tree sitting beside her door, at the end of a trail of soil that led down the corridor and, presumably, to the foyer where she'd seen the plants yesterday. "And what's the tree doing here?"

The prawn person grunted and uncurled as he rolled over. "I told you yesterday. I'm Jay Felix, at your service, and today I come with bonus pants." He waved at his shorts. "I'm looking for the woman who fits these remarkably delicate shoes." Tucked into the crook of his other arm were the heels she'd ditched yesterday in her haste to run away. But there was pink fur on them that she didn't remember. Pink, fluffy, pale…oh!

Her gaze raked the fluffy handcuff wrapped around Jay's wrist and followed the chain to the other cuff encircling the tree's trunk. "Why are you handcuffed to that poor tree?"

"Sapling. Not really a tree yet." Jay – Jason? – winced as he sat up. "The new resort manager threatened to have me removed from the island if I didn't leave you alone. She seems to think I'm dangerous. So I handcuffed myself to a tree and promised to stay put. The tree was in the foyer then, though. And I was worried about you, so I figured I'd take the tree for a walk and wait here instead."

None of this made sense. Her head started throbbing.

"Jason…Jay…"

"Take your pick. Most people call me Jay, but you're different."

"Where are the cameras?" she whispered, looking for hidden lenses.

"I got one on my phone, if you want to take selfies.

Give me a sec to get up. I'll take one of both of us together. First couple moment and all." He unfastened the wrist cuff and rose, pulling his phone out of his pocket as he pulled her to his side. "Smile."

Phuong did her best, but the phone only photographed how badly she'd failed. She looked slightly manic, her eyes showing her desperate desire to run again. She'd had enough of being a laughing stock. Shrugging out of his grasp, she took a step back. "I'm sorry, I know this is just a joke to you, but I don't find it funny. Please, I just want a coffee and maybe a glimpse of the beach. Then I'll go."

"Don't." His tone sounded too serious. "Please don't. Spend a day with me. That's all I ask. Just one day. Please, Phuong."

She started when he said her name. How could Jason, the man her mind had desperately clung to in its hope to get her safely out of hell, be Jay Felix? "How do you know my name?"

She expected a flippant comment about how she'd told him yesterday, but he surprised her.

"You told me, weeks ago. Made me write it on my belly and take photos. It was a fucking permanent marker, too. Took days to wash off."

Phuong cracked a smile. "You volunteered to do it. I didn't make you."

"Really?" He squinted at her. "I guess I could've. I might've had a bit of bourbon before I did it, too."

Drunk. She'd pinned her hopes on a drunkard who didn't remember. "Doesn't matter. Joke's on me now, I guess." Tears formed so fast she couldn't stop them from falling. "Shit, sorry, I – "

"Tissues." He seized her hand and towed her along the corridor. "Get the lady some tissues!" he bellowed.

A few seconds later, a box appeared in front of her. Phuong grabbed a handful. She wiped her face, blew her nose and whispered, "Thank you." She glanced at Jay, staring out the window at the boat dock. "Where's good for coffee?"

"I'll take you to the restaurant," he replied and held open the door.

Phuong wanted to protest, but her stomach snarled so she subsided. She hoped she had enough money to cover the cost of her coffee.

Jay led the way to the deserted restaurant and threw the doors open for her. "Where do you want to sit?"

An annoyed-looking waitress appeared. "I'm sorry, sir, the restaurant's closed between ten and twelve. Come back at twelve for lunch or there are vending machines – "

Jay folded his arms. "Good. Then we won't be disturbed and we won't have to wait long. Call it a private function for two. We'll sit – " he glanced around and pointed at a table in the centre of the room – "there. Unless you want to sit somewhere else?" He glanced at Phuong.

Phuong wished she could shrink out of sight. She wanted no part of this confrontation.

"Sir, you don't understand – "

"No, you don't understand. I own the hotel. I'd like breakfast for two served in the restaurant, but if that's too much trouble for you, fine. We'll have a private table set in the ocean function room. I'll need a waitress, personal chef, plus a barista because the lady wants a coffee. For the next two hours, plus whatever time it takes you to clean up afterwards." He stared down the waitress, showing no sign of blinking. "What'll it be, Tiffany? Don't make this any harder than it has to be."

Tiffany bowed her head. "Yes, sir, breakfast for two, coming up."

"Now, wait a minute. You didn't ask what we wanted for breakfast. I'd like some of those pastries you put out on the buffet every morning. With fruit. How about you, Phuong? You got a preference?"

She shook her head frantically.

"Fine. Enough of whatever for two, then. Did you understand that, Tiffany? Or do you need me to repeat it, just to make sure?'"

"I understand, sir." Tiffany kept her eyes on the floor. Just like Phuong had learned to do with Norman.

Phuong felt sick. Not another one. A demanding bully who'd crush her just as badly, but this time she wouldn't get up again. Couldn't do it again. The door loomed in front of her, but she slammed it open and kept running.

"Phuong! Wait!" Heavy footfalls followed her and she knew she couldn't run forever. He'd reach out and grab her and hurt her and…

But he didn't. He didn't touch her, just kept pace one step behind her.

She whirled to face him. "No. What you just did to her was horrible. No one should be bullied like that. Not ever."

Jay laughed. Just like that, the bastard laughed at her deepest fears. "Her? Tiffany the restaurant manager is a drill sergeant who makes life hell for waitstaff, kitchenhands and chefs alike. You ask any of the staff who work with her. I've heard plenty of complaints, but I never ate in the restaurant, so I didn't meet her until today. You know what she does in her two hour break? Hides in her office and watches daytime TV. Reruns or talk shows from the US. And if anyone interrupts her, they end up scraping and washing dishes for a week. She finds fault with everyone. One girl ended up on stress leave after Tiffany screamed at her for not picking food up from the floor and serving it to someone. No joke, it was plated wrong and the chef hadn't noticed. When the girl grabbed it, the ribs just slithered to the floor, and the next thing she knew, Tiffany was screaming like a banshee. She was sleeping with Meier, the old manager, too, so he turned a deaf ear to all the complaints. You'd be amazed at some of the dodgy stuff that goes on behind the scenes here." He winked. "I'll take you 'round by her office window and you can peek in to see what she's doing. Watching TV, not working. She's pissed because I'm making her work instead of watching *The Boring and the Botoxed* or whatever it's called. Honest."

She wasn't sure what to believe. One minute he was a bullying bastard, and the next, he was the man she'd exchanged emails with and driven for thousands of kilometres to meet. One who could save her from…everything. "I'm confused. I don't know what to believe any more."

He grinned. "That's why you need coffee. Let's talk over breakfast at Tiffany's." Something made him grimace, but he didn't say any more as he headed inside.

Phuong sighed. She'd come this far. What else could she do but follow him?

THIRTY-SIX

Jason drummed his fingers on the table as one of Tiffany's subordinates served breakfast and coffee. He willed the woman to leave, but she insisted on setting everything out on the table like their own private buffet. Couldn't she see the girl was ready to bolt? Every second she sat there, the hunted look in her eyes grew more and more pronounced. He'd do anything to make up for the mess he'd made yesterday. And he'd start…if only the waitress would take the hint and leave.

"Will there be anything else, sir?"

He shook his head. "We'll shout if we need you."

The waitress marched back to the kitchen.

As soon as they had the restaurant to themselves, Jason leaned across the table and whispered, "It was the frog, wasn't it? I went a bit too far for you with the frog-kissing. That's why you ran yesterday."

Phuong choked on her coffee.

"Are you all right?"

She flashed two thumbs-up and nodded in between coughing.

Jason eyed her for a moment before he was sure she wasn't going to die, then continued, "Look, I had it all planned out. I wanted to show you me at my best. The whole package. I was all set to offer you the night of your life, as a sample of what to expect. Dancing all night and all that. But then I saw you and you looked so scared, all I wanted to do was wrap my arms around you and make it all okay. So I got sort of flustered and I said the first thing that came to mind, the bit about kissing frogs, and you ran and…fuck." She had that look again – the one from yesterday. Right before she took off. "Say something. Is it the whole frog thing in general, or just that you don't kiss frogs on a first date?"

Phuong's tongue darted out and licked her lips. "I don't know anything about frogs. I…I just can't get the image out of my head. One minute I was nervously knocking on the door, then you introduced yourself as some rock star, and when I wanted to look anywhere but at your face as I tried to understand what you were saying, I saw you were…your…" Words failed her, so she pointed under the table.

Jason grinned. "Giving you a full salute, no less. I thanked every lucky star I knew of yesterday. You looked hot in that red dress and those heels…fuck, I'd like to see you in those again. Just the heels and nothing else."

Phuong froze. She lowered her gaze into her lap. "Please, I'd prefer not to talk about it. Yesterday or sex. I don't..."

He waited for her to finish, but when it seemed she wasn't going to, he blurted out the burning question: "Are you a virgin? Have you never seen a man naked before?"

That made her laugh. "Oh no. And no! I've seen plenty...had plenty...well, not a lot but..." She paled. "You just looked so big and intimidating. I was already scared and...well, it's huge, and I'm...I'm not sure I can..."

"You're scared of my cock? Aww, you'll hurt his feelings. Don't you worry. The bigger, the better, you'll see. We'll take it slow the first time. And the second...I'll let you call the pace." Another wink as he tried to hide his sigh of relief. Yeah, he'd done virgins, but he preferred a bit of experience. No self-respecting rock star would go looking for a virgin. Too much trouble by half.

"But not...not until after we're married." Phuong lifted her chin as if she thought it would emphasise her point. "Wedding first."

Good thing he didn't plan on a long engagement.

"Sure. How's Friday sound?"

Her jaw dropped. "What?"

"I guess I should've done this first." Jason eased off his chair and knelt on the carpet. "Phuong, will you marry me?"

She stared at him for a bloody long time. Too long. "Are you joking?" she asked finally.

His knees hurt and she'd left him hanging. This wasn't funny. "No."

"I barely know you. I don't even know what to call you." She was ready to run, he could see it.

"My name's Jason. Jason, Jay, baby, rock star...fuck, marry me, and you can make up your own damn pet names and trademark them. Take your pick." Just as long as she didn't say no. He wasn't sure what he'd do if she said that.

Phuong wet her lips. So scared, so vulnerable…he just wanted to wrap his arms around her and comfort her, all while she was driving him crazy. "Jason. I can't answer that. I know almost nothing about you."

"You're not saying no, right?"

Slowly, she nodded. "I just…you said to give you a day. Could you give me a day, too?"

"Sure." He climbed stiffly back onto his chair and grabbed a pastry. "Right, so what do you want to know?"

THIRTY-SEVEN

The basket of Danish pastries held nothing but crumbs, though the taste of cherry still lingered on Phuong's tongue. She wasn't sure how many cups of coffee she'd consumed, but she was still surprised to see that she and Jason had been talking for so long that they weren't the only customers in the restaurant any more. Maybe a third of the tables were occupied and, even more surprising, no one was staring at Jason. He'd always had long hair in the pictures she'd seen of him, so perhaps the shorter style he now sported was enough of a disguise.

They'd discussed parents, siblings and pets, movies and music and even books, though he'd done more listening than talking when it came to books. Under the watchful eyes of her father and brother, she hadn't dared to read anything more graphic than young adult fiction back home, but she'd developed a taste for them, all the same. Girls in the first blush of love and boys in their first moody obsession, driven to be adults and yet clinging desperately to their childhood while life pushed them further out into the world of decisions they didn't have the experience to make wisely.

As if she knew what she was doing now.

They'd both skirted the most important question: who marries a stranger they've only just met?

She'd been businesslike and upfront about it with Norman, and look where that had gotten her.

But the more time she spent with Jason, the more she wondered whether she should tell him her reasons at all. Somehow along the way, this had become more than just a business deal to her. Otherwise, she'd have agreed to marry him in a heartbeat. The sooner she got her citizenship, the better, after all. But now she wanted more. She wanted him, too – wanted his heart the way she'd already given up hers.

A man she didn't know! His every movement, every nuance of his facial expression, were all new to her, yet she found herself memorising every one. In case this was all she had with him.

She wasn't the sort of girl to entice a rock star. She could barely hold his attention now, with him glancing around the room with increasing frequency.

No, wait – he was looking at her expectantly.

"What?"

"I said, d'you want to go somewhere more private? How about that walk on the beach I promised you?" He peered under the table. "I think the thongs I bought you will be too big for your feet, but I can swing by the gift shop and see if maybe..."

"I'll be fine," she assured him with a nervous smile.

They made their way out of the restaurant and followed the sound of distant waves to a beach of endless sand.

"Low tide," Jason explained, pointing. "Give it a few hours. The waves will be breaking where we are now. Hard to believe, but there won't be a crab in sight, either. All these will be safely hidden in their little crabholes in the sand."

Crabs? Phuong didn't see any of them, until she realised that the speckled sand was moving…and the movement wasn't sand at all but armies of tiny crabs, waging war against one another, or fleeing from Jason's huge, tramping feet. A million tiny claws, scurrying and pinching and…

Warm fingers touched her hand. "Hey, it's all right. They're more scared of us than we are of them. Their pincers aren't big enough to hurt you. And if any of them think to try…" He ripped the thong off his foot and slapped the rubber sole on his palm. "I'm your knight in shining armour. I'll protect you from crabs."

Phuong couldn't help laughing. The weight on her heart lifted. Maybe she could see her way clear to a happy future. The more she worried about her decision, the greater the chance this opportunity would vanish altogether. What did she have to lose? Her self-respect? Norman had ripped that away from her a long time ago, if she'd ever really had any in the first place. Why wait any longer?

"Yes," she said.

"Yes, I'm allowed to be your knight in shining armour? Great. I'll have to commission some armour. I draw the line at horses, though. Seems a bit weird, riding something so huge with a mind of its own. I mean, what's to stop the horse from saying, 'I'm bigger than you, and you're bloody heavy. Fuck this. I'm not carrying you anywhere,' and just throwing you off like a carton of empty beer cans and galloping off to find – "

Phuong took a deep breath, no longer paying attention to Jason's rambling. "Yes, I'll marry you."

For a moment, he was speechless, but it didn't last long. "Thank fuck for that. I'll take you into town for rings and clothes and shit tomorrow. We'll do the church on Friday." He waved up and down his clothed body. "Two days and all this will be yours. Unless you want a sample earlier? I'm all for try before you buy." He flashed a cheeky grin.

Phuong's heart fluttered at the thought as her memory favoured her with a flashback of what he kept under his clothes. She was definitely getting the better end of the deal and she knew it. "No, I can wait," she replied. It's not like she had the first idea of what to do with a man's body, as Norman had frequently told her. Perhaps Jason would be willing to show her.

After they were married, though. If he knew how bad she was in bed, the marriage would be off in a moment. She definitely didn't want that.

THIRTY-EIGHT

For the first time in months, Jason woke with the dawn. He made short work of a shower and shave. He even shrugged into a shirt before his watch told him it was 8 am. He killed twenty minutes by skimming through one of his library books: the one with the wedding in it, of course. He hadn't been to many weddings; the ones he'd crashed had been publicity stunts for adoring fans. He'd arrived, performed a song or two, posed for some photos with the couple before grabbing a drink and getting the fuck out of there. Sheila's was different because she was family, a cousin of some kind, and he'd been so off his face from the previous night's concert afterparty that he couldn't even remember the fangirl's name. Or if she gave good head.

Didn't matter. The only name he needed to remember now was Phuong's, because tomorrow she'd be his wife.

Hear that, Angel and Audra and Jo and everyone else

out there? He'd be happily married to his blushing bride. They'd have a fucking fairy tale ending.

He had a list, though. One he'd made with Phuong on the table at dinner last night. He'd have liked to make other things with her on the table, but he'd agreed to wait until after tomorrow. It's not like his dick would fall off in the meantime. At least, he hoped it wouldn't.

The list. Couldn't have a wedding without the list, which read:

DRESS

SHOES

RINGS

JEWELLERY

Funny. She'd said that the only jewellery they needed was the rings – why write it twice? – but Jason had laughed and left it on the list. If Jo was anything to go by, every outfit needed matching shoes and jewellery. Especially for a wedding. He wouldn't know the first thing about picking shit that matched, but he hoped Phuong would.

He couldn't wait any more. Throwing the book down, he headed out to Reception. No need to take the hidden jungle track this time. He marched proudly down the main path, past the other villas to the foyer where he expected he'd have to wait for her, but he was wrong.

Phuong sat primly in one of the woven armchairs, from her glossy, tied-back hair to her hands (carefully clasped in her lap) right down to her side-by-side shoes. She flashed him a nervous smile when he entered, which flustered him more than anything.

He wanted to stride forward, to take her in his arms and dip her for a passionate kiss, but something in her expression stopped him. If he didn't know better, he'd swear it was fear, but how could anyone be afraid of him?

"You ready to go?" he said instead.

Phuong nodded and rose stiffly. "As ready as I'll ever be." She headed for the doors leading out to the main jetty.

One of the maintenance guys trundled a wheelbarrow down the jetty, full of something red, black and grey. Jason moved closer to the window to get a closer look at the wheelbarrow's contents. As it bumped over the uneven boards, a tail flopped out of the mess. A shark's tail. That meant…shark skin, shark bones or whatever it had, and bloody shark guts. The maintenance guy tipped the carved-up carcass into the ocean, turning the water red. Blood…oh fuck.

Jason turned away, fighting to keep his breakfast down. No way was he going anywhere near the dead shark. "Where are you going? The helipad's this way." As if to punctuate his point, the thumping beat of a helicopter rose to a crescendo as it swooped over the building.

Just like that, her fear was gone. Phuong wore a genuine smile. "We're flying?"

"Fuck yeah. I'm not driving that hell road after it tried to kill me. Enough to terrify me, that's for sure. Killer cows and crazy cops and that dominatrix matron…you wouldn't believe me if I told you." He shivered at the memory, then realised the receptionist was staring at him. "You coming or what?"

To his surprise, she crossed the room and took his hand. He didn't say anything. He just folded his fingers around her much smaller ones and held them securely. It was a start, and a promising one, too.

He didn't let go until he'd helped her into the helicopter and had to hoist himself into the tiny cabin. Sliding into the seat beside Phuong, he asked, "So, ever flown in one of these before?"

She shook her head. "Just jet planes. This is a lot smaller." She stared up at the rotors. "It's hard to believe something so small can stay in the air."

"No, what's hard to believe is that jets can fly," Shou interjected, swinging easily into the cockpit. "Huge hunks of metal, engines bigger than my baby here." He stroked the hatch before slamming it shut. "This skims almost as gracefully as the big black kites you see soaring overhead. Well, on the mainland, anyway. You don't get as many of them out here. The ospreys and sea eagles don't like them."

Phuong nodded politely and subsided.

Jason felt a flash of anger that the pilot had silenced her just when she'd started to open up. The man had no idea how hard it was to…

Her hand slipped into his, then squeezed. Jason met her worried glance. "Nervous flier?"

She nodded. "I like it better than boats, mostly because I don't get seasick in the air, but I don't really like flying."

Her grip tightened as they started their ascent, slowly cutting off the circulation to Jason's fingers as the helicopter headed south-west to fly down the Dampier Peninsula and cross Cable Beach before angling in to land at the airport in the middle of town. He waited until Phuong's full attention – and both her hands – were occupied with her headphones and seatbelt before he tried to shake the tingles out of his hand as blood flow painfully returned.

At least he wasn't the only thing she was afraid of. Boats and flying. But she'd come to the island by boat, and flown to the mainland with him. Maybe she'd manage to conquer her fear of him, soon, too. Fuck, he hoped so. Every time he saw her tongue touch her lips, he wanted to taste her, to tell her that she had nothing to be nervous about because he'd protect her from all of it and…and…something stopped him.

The pilot escorted them off the tarmac and into the tiny office that doubled as a departure and arrival lounge. "Give me a call when you need a lift home."

Jason nodded and led Phuong outside to the taxi rank.

"Where to?" the driver asked.

"Wherever you can get a wedding dress in this town." Jason climbed into the back seat after Phuong, only to find the driver staring at him. "What?" Of course he'd autograph something. As soon as the man asked him to. Any time now…

"This is Broome, mate. No bridal shops here. The nearest one's probably in Darwin or Perth. You're better off hopping back on a plane for that 'cause I'm not driving to Darwin."

Jason recovered quickly. "Fine. Then…whatever the best dress shop here is." He glanced at Phuong. She nodded with what looked like resignation, which only irritated him. "Look, if you can't find anything decent here, I'll fly you to Perth, Darwin, wherever. Whatever you want."

"Jason." Even the way she whispered his name did things to his insides. How did she do that? Most girls only stirred a response from his cock, not the rest of him. "Jason, I can't afford a new dress. Not a proper wedding dress or anything. I spent the last money I had on fuel to get to you. I have enough money for a coffee. Maybe. But not—"

He extracted a credit card from his wallet and threw it into her lap. "Use that, then."

She shook her head. "Jason, I can't."

"Sure you can. Tomorrow, you're going to become my wife, which means half of what I own is yours. It's a dress for tomorrow, when that money's yours already. I probably owe you for petrol, too. You should have told me you were coming so I could pay for your flights or however you wanted to travel." He pulled out his phone and held it up so she could see the screen, then tapped out a sequence of numbers. "That's the PIN for that card. Keep it. I'll call the bank on Monday and get them to send you out your own cards, but that should do you until then. If not, just let me know."

"This is Chinatown. Most of the clothes shops are here, or you can go to the shopping centre on the other side of the airport," the taxi driver announced.

Jason paid him and found himself standing beside Phuong on the footpath outside a frock shop, whatever that was. It had dresses in the window display, though, and one of them definitely had her attention.

Jason took a deep breath and inhaled the scent of fresh-brewed beans. "I'll just go get a coffee. You want me to grab one for you, too?"

Phuong nodded and entered the shop. The door squeaked shut behind her, safely enclosing her in the air-conditioned cavern. She'd be safe for a few minutes, Jason decided, slipping around the corner to the café.

184

THIRTY-NINE

Bells chimed as Phuong entered the shop, announcing her arrival more musically than she expected.

"Can I help you?" the shop assistant asked. Her name tag announced that her name was Betty.

Phuong thought of the credit card burning a hole in her pocket. "I guess so. I need a dress to wear for a wedding tomorrow."

"What do you have in mind? Anything catch your eye?"

Phuong pointed at the window display. "I want to try that one. I'm thinking…red." When she'd been a little girl, dreaming about her future wedding, she'd always imagined herself in red like the brides back home. Would Jason want her to wear white, like a traditional Australian bride? She'd have to ask him when he returned. Not that this shop had anything that looked like a formal wedding dress.

Betty nodded. "What size?"

Phuong told her.

"Right. I'll put this in the change room for you while you have a look around. See if anything else takes your fancy."

It had been months since she last did any clothes shopping, so Phuong picked several possible dresses before inspecting the sale rack. Who knew how long it would be before Jason let her come into town again? She could hardly wear overpriced t-shirts and board-shorts from the resort gift shop all the time. Selecting a few sale items that looked like her size, she headed for the change rooms.

Phuong undressed and reached for the first hanger when she caught sight of her reflection. She'd lost weight living with Norman, that was for sure – she could see her ribs for the first time in years. It wasn't like she'd been doing much exercise, stuck in that tiny flat, but she'd been too nervous to eat most of the time. That much hadn't changed – she hadn't eaten today, either, but that was mostly because she knew the boat trip would bring it all back up again.

Maybe she'd get a muffin or something once she was done dress shopping.

Smiling, she slipped the first dress over her head. Red satin with white polka dots.

It hung off her, showing every angle while obliterating the curves she did have. No way.

Next. What was with the polka dots this season? Had she missed some event where the Duchess of Cambridge wore polka dots, and now everyone had to? This one was emerald green, though, not red.

Ugh. It flared out nicely around her hips, then narrowed

again and made it hard to walk. Not to mention it made her look like she had no breasts at all.

White with seagulls. Phuong's fingers fastened the silver buttons – so many of them, all the way up – before she examined her reflection. Well, it fitted and showed that she had a figure, but white…she set it aside to show Jason, in case he insisted on making her look like a virginal bride.

The same dress again, but chequered in red and white like a tablecloth. Oh, sure, it would fit but…Norman would have approved. Buttons for easy access while matching that hideously cheerful vinyl tablecloth his mother had bought him. No. Absolutely not.

One with a red floral print. It flattened her boobs again and reminded her of her mother's favourite curtains. It could have been cut from the same cloth. No. She wouldn't get married in a tablecloth or curtains. She was a woman, not a window.

Plain red this time, which Phuong slipped over her head carefully, hoping this one would do. The tiny sleeves slid down her shoulders and sat on her arms like something out of the 1980s. No way on Earth was she wearing a wedding dress that made her look like one of her mother's bridesmaids.

That left one last dress. The one from the window display, of course. Which would look nothing like it had on the shop mannequin, so she'd be wearing seagulls to her wedding. Flying scavengers on white. If that's what Jason wanted…

Phuong slid the red dress over her head and arched back to fasten the zip. There. A perfect fit. The darts in the front made her breasts look bigger – always a plus – and the skirt flared out from her waist, like one of those dresses fairy tale princesses wore, but this was more practical, ending just below the knee. It was exactly the same colour as her favourite heels, too, so that was one thing less to buy.

No, it wasn't a formal wedding dress, but she wanted to be married in this one. It felt…right, somehow.

She pulled the elastic out of her hair and let it cascade loose over her back. Up or down? She didn't want a veil — not that she'd be able to find one here — but having her hair down would feel a little like having a veil. Maybe…

"How are you going in there? You right for sizes?"

"Fine, thank you."

"Found the one yet?"

"Yes, I think so." If Jason approved. If he didn't…

"Let's see it, then."

With trembling hands, Phuong unlocked the dressing room door and stepped out. Betty pointed at the trio of mirrors lined up against the wall, angled to give her a good view from all sides. Now she could definitely see this dress suited her better than it had fitted the mannequin. What were the chances?

"Beautiful, don't you think?" Betty asked.

Phuong opened her mouth to thank her for the compliment.

"Of course she is," Jason drawled. "I won't be able to look at anyone else tomorrow. Not that I'd want to." He gulped from his coffee cup, not taking his eyes off her.

Phuong's cheeks flamed with a blush that rivalled the brightness of her dress. "You…like it?"

"The dress looks good on you. It's a pretty dress." Another gulp of coffee. "I like the red. Bright and different and…perfect. Yeah. You look beautiful." He drained the cup.

Phuong's heart froze. No man had ever called her beautiful before. Norman had called her hot on the day they met, his eyes wearing that half-lidded look she'd soon learned meant he was thinking about sex. Jason's expression was different, though. More wonder and less lust. Definitely not what she was used to, and she wasn't sure what to make of it.

Norman had made her feel like an army of tiny crabs were crawling across her skin, a precursor to panic and pain. Acquisitive, possessive, hungry.

Jason made her forget everything — what she was wearing, where she stood, even who she was — because all she could think of was him, and wonder what he was thinking. He could have any woman he wanted. He would have her tomorrow, but he'd still called her beautiful, and the sincerity in his eyes said it was true. She stood a little taller at the thought. Tomorrow night, she'd stand before him without the dress, naked even, and she'd be wholly his. Would his eyes express the same approval then?

"I should get dressed," she said softly and retreated into the change room.

FORTY

"What sort of jewellery goes with that?" Jason asked in what he hoped was a casual tone, nodding at the red dress Phuong would wear in his fantasies forever. Well, where she wore anything, of course.

"I have just the thing," the shop assistant said, her eyes shining. She reached into a glass cabinet and snagged a necklace made of white beads, coated in something shiny that made them look like pearls.

Jason reached for the price tag. No way those were pearls. Plastic, maybe.

He glanced at Phuong. He recognised the blank expression – his sister, Jo, did it well. With Jo, it meant that he had to stop what he was doing, right now, or the moment they were alone she'd rip him a new one, and he'd add one more thing to the mysterious list of What Not To Do Around Women Unless You Want To Lose Your Balls.

Buying cheap jewellery was already on that list.

"No, thanks." He managed a grin for the shop assistant.

Her face fell while Phuong hid her smile.

Victory!

A few minutes later, they left the shop. He swung her bag of purchases, wondering what else she'd bought, and asked, "So, what's next? Shoes? Jeweller?"

Phuong stopped sipping her coffee. "I already have shoes. We should get the rings next." She ducked her head. "If we're still going ahead tomorrow."

"Why wouldn't we be? I'm not backing out. Are you?" He stared at her in panic. She couldn't do that to him. Not her. She wouldn't be that cruel.

"Of course not. I just…this is all so fast. It's hard to believe that tomorrow we'll be…married."

"Sure is. Can't believe my luck," he replied cheerfully. Thank fuck for that. "Jewellers. Dampier Terrace. Just down the lane. They'll have what we need." And a wedding present for her, too. He crossed his fingers and hoped he'd gotten this one right.

The first shop wasn't as much a jeweller as a pearl showroom, with huge display cases of jewellery, loose pearls and all sorts of things made out of mother-of-pearl. Including a selection of caviar spoons, sitting in a polished oyster shell dish. As if anyone would use such a tiny spoon. Actually, the hotel manager, Meier, might. Ah, but the manager wasn't Meier any more. It was that angry English chick.

But she didn't matter right now. Nobody did but Phuong, who'd headed straight for the section with the most spotlights directed on it. He might not be an expert at marketing, but all that time spent on stage had taught him a thing or two. The spotlights focussed the audience's attention on where you wanted it to be – on the star, the singer or, on the rare occasion, the soloist. Whatever that display held, it was the crown jewels of the shop's collection.

He hung back and watched. Phuong peered through the sparkling glass, then her eyes widened. She took a step back. Her attention turned to a nearby case that was only slightly less well-lit. A moment later, she stiffened and walked away.

"Can I help you, sir?"

Jason turned and met a familiar face. Now, if only he could remember when…

"Did she send you back for the matching bracelet after all?" The woman smiled. "We still have it." She gestured toward the second display unit Phuong had rejected.

This was where Jo had bought her necklace. A strand of round, silvery pearls. Smaller than the plastic necklace in the dress shop, but…

"No," he replied. "I want something that goes with this." He held open the dress bag. "And a ring to match. Do you have men's rings?"

Her smile widened. "Come with me, sir." She led him to the display units set into the counter.

Jason glanced at Phuong, who was intent on the contents of a cabinet on the opposite wall. He'd check those in a minute. Ring first.

"These are the men's rings." She lifted out a tray that held fewer rings than he had fingers. "See anything you like, sir?" She tilted the tray.

One of the rings winked at him. Well, that's what it

looked like. On closer examination, he realised it was a gold-coloured stone set in the band. "What's that?"

"A champagne diamond from the mine up north, near Lake Argyle. Our jeweller likes to source stones locally," she said smoothly.

Champagne diamonds. They sounded right for a wedding. Celebrating and all that shit. Jason nodded. "Yeah. That one. Show me women's rings with those, then."

Of course, there were dozens of those, all winking and sparkling at him like they knew he was out of his depth. Fucking rocks. Time to call for help.

"Hey, Phuong. Which one of these do you want?"

The startled shop assistant recovered quickly, hitching her smile back into place. "Is the young lady with you, sir?"

"Yes." Phuong's soft voice behind him didn't sound particularly certain.

"Yes," Jason repeated, with a pointed look for the woman. "Show her the rings. And the necklaces, too. Just like the one I bought my sister."

"Your sister?" She tittered and winked. "Ah, yes, sir." She pulled out her keys and headed for the necklace cabinet.

"Do you bring all your girlfriends here?" Phuong asked.

Jason couldn't stand the sadness in her eyes. "No. The only time I came here was with my sister. My real sister. The one who used to steal my Lego blocks when we were little so she could build stables for her toy ponies. Now part owner of Romance Island Resort, though I still own the rest." He sighed. "She understands business better than I do. Been to uni and all. Got her degree. She helped me out when I first took over the place. She said she wanted pearls as payment. I swear she picked the most expensive necklace as payback for those ponies."

"What did you do to them?"

"Don't remember. I grabbed my blocks and the ponies and hid them. By the time she noticed, I couldn't remember where I put them. They're probably still hidden in our parents' old house." He grinned at the memory.

"My brother used to steal my toys, too. I always knew his hiding places, though, so I got them back again later."

A thought struck him. "Do you want to invite your brother to the wedding tomorrow? I can arrange flights."

"No!"

Her vehemence surprised him. He opened his mouth to ask more, but the woman returned with several necklaces and a tray of rings, so he closed it again.

Phuong stared at the rings for a long time, until Jason finally lost patience and pointed at the biggest, most ostentatious one he could see, all pearls and sparkly bits tangled in what resembled gold seaweed. "Try that one on," he insisted.

The monstrous ring covered half her finger, right up to her knuckle. Jason burst out laughing. Phuong cracked a smile as she took it off.

"How about that one?" She pointed at a delicate ring set with one tiny pearl.

"No." He bit his lip. "Maybe you should pick a necklace first. Something to go with your dress."

The shop assistant edged one forward, still fastened around the neck of the headless velvet display stand. "This is the finest white pearl strand in the store at the moment. With exceptionally high lustre, as you can see — "

"We'll take it," Jason interrupted.

"No." Phuong shook her head violently. "I can't."

Jason didn't understand. "Are you allergic to pearls or something?"

She shuddered. "No. That necklace…the price of that necklace is more than my university fees for a year. Fees, board, everything. I can't wear something that expensive around my neck when there are better things to spend the money on."

Jason shrugged. "So pay your fees. You got my credit card. Let me know if you need more. I'll sort it out." He turned back to the shiny things laid out on the counter. "So, are you going to pick a ring or make me do it?"

FORTY-ONE

The next hour passed in a daze for Phuong. She slid ring after ring on her finger, seeing the sparkle of an endless procession of diamonds until Jason held one up that he insisted suited her best. She nodded, too stunned to argue.

Her uni fees – he'd pay them, just like that. No need for citizenship, the wedding, any of it…except that the only reason he'd given her the money was because tomorrow she would become his wife.

She had to tell him. She couldn't take his money like that when there was no need. And when she came clean, maybe he'd tell her why a man like him was looking for a partner on an email-order bride website.

He wasn't Norman. He was nothing like Norman. Everything would be okay, she told herself as her stomach churned in consternation.

"I don't know about you, but I'm starving. Breakfast

feels like forever ago. Have you ever had chocolate chip pancakes?" His boyish grin was contagious.

"No, I haven't," she whispered.

"Too hot to walk, so we'll get a cab." He hailed one and she climbed into the back seat. A few minutes later, the taxi came to a halt. She staggered out again into cloying heat. Gentle hands righted her. "Don't worry, I'll get you inside with a cold drink in just a minute."

Dizziness blurred her vision as Jason half-carried her into coolness, followed by hardness as his arms gave way to…wood? A chair cradled her while Jason knelt on the floor at her feet.

"Drink, baby."

Something hard pressed to her lips. Damp. Drink. She gulped down the water, feeling some of it running down her chin, but she didn't care. With coolness came clarity. They were in a restaurant with dark wooden floors below and whizzing fans overhead. Just like some of the old places back in Singapore.

"Better?" Jason asked, his forehead creased with concern.

She nodded limply.

He rose and took the seat across the table from her. "When did you last eat?"

Phuong thought hard. "Dinner?"

He tapped the menu in front of her. "Pick something. Anything. You need to eat."

She had to tell him. Stomach twisting, threatening to throw out anything she put in it until she told him. "Not hungry."

Jason waved a waitress over and ordered something, but

Phuong wasn't listening any more. Not until his hand touched hers did she dare to raise her eyes to his face.

"What is it? What did I do wrong?" he asked. "Everything was fine until the jewellery shop and then you went all distant. So tell me what I did wrong."

"Nothing. You did nothing wrong," Phuong responded, but her voice sounded dead. "It's just…you don't need to pay for my fees or buy me expensive jewellery. You don't need to do anything for me."

"But I want to."

She tried again. "I created a profile on that website because I needed an Australian husband to help me pay my fees so I can finish my degree. This would be my final year and I don't – "

His smile died. "You don't have the money. You already told me that. So you're marrying me for my money, is that what you're saying?" So cold. Now he was the distant one. She didn't blame him.

"No. All I wanted was an Australian husband. One who could help me get my citizenship so I could get a government loan. It would take a couple of years, but I'd still be able to finish my degree. I'll be a good wife, I swear…"

One warm hand enveloped hers, stopping her from wringing them.

"But that's two years of your life. It sounds like pretty poor pay for two years, however light the work. So if I give you the money for your university fees now, no strings attached, what will you do? Will you go home, go back to university? What?" His eyes captured hers. She couldn't look away.

Tears filled her eyes. "I don't know," she whispered.

"Do you want to marry me?"

"Yes." This came out louder, firmer.

Those honey eyes examined her soul, weighing it, as she desperately hoped she wouldn't be found wanting.

"Pay it now." He pushed his phone across the table. "Go to your university website, and pay your fees with my credit card. The one I gave you this morning. Do it."

She stared at him, stricken. "I can't take your money like that."

"Then I'll go back and buy those pearls for you. Or I'll call the university and have a scholarship created with your name on it. Just do it."

With shaking fingers, she swiped through several screens until she found the phone's web browser and logged into the university's payment page. She lost count of the number of times she had to backspace before she'd entered the credit card number correctly. Seconds passed while the payment processed, then a message popped up, telling her the payment was accepted. "It's done." She wasn't sure whether to laugh or cry. "Thank you so much."

"Show me." He held out his hand for the phone and she surrendered it. He checked the screen, nodded, then tucked it back into his pocket. "Right, it's not hypothetical any more. You've paid for your degree. That's not an issue any more. Now, what are you going to do?"

"I still don't know, because it's not just about me," she said steadily. "What about you? Why did you create a profile on an email-order bride website? If we go ahead with this wedding tomorrow, what do you want out of this marriage?"

"I want my wife to be happy," he said simply.

"There must be more than that. A reason, something driving you to…it can't be that simple! Life isn't that simple."

Jason shrugged. "Why not? I believe I can make you happy. I'll do my best to keep you that way. I know you'll make me happy. Happily ever after, just like the fairy tales. Yeah, they leave out a bit of the detail, but it's essentially the same. I went on that website looking for a woman who believes in fairy tales. I found you. It's fate, Phuong. Let's follow it and see where it takes us. I promise I'll make sure you enjoy the ride."

Phuong didn't know what to say. Fortunately, she was saved by a waitress carrying two plates of pancakes.

Jason waited until the woman left before adding, "Marry me tomorrow. Not for my money, not for my citizenship, but because you're willing to give us a shot at happiness together with the whole fairy tale."

She held his gaze for what felt like forever. This was the offer of a lifetime. No matter how much it scared her, she had to follow her heart. "I will."

FORTY-TWO

Jason rapped on Phuong's door, curling his lip at the pathetic sound of his knuckles tapping glass. Now, if it had been a proper wooden door, he could've produced a much more manly knock, the sort that echoed through the room and announced his presence. One that said, "Your husband is here," instead of some pathetic loser whose knock sounded like an apology for his very presence.

Kind of like the difference between tapping your glass with a knife to get a room's attention or just raising your voice and letting out an almighty, "Oi!" He wasn't one to pussyfoot around, but he didn't want to break Phuong's door, either. She was just so fragile, ready to shatter into a million pieces if he did the wrong thing. And he didn't intend to screw this up. It was his wedding day, for fuck's sake.

He tapped again. "Phuong? It's me. This is your

morning wake up call, like I promised. Even though it's not really morning any more. Your chariot awaits, so I've come to collect you and escort you to – "

The door slid open with a blissful sigh, and Jason could see why.

Her eyes looked bigger, darker, but warmer, too, like he'd done something right yesterday, and that's why she'd stayed. Could she want this as much as he did? He sure hoped so.

Strawberries. Her lips looked like strawberries, ripe and sweet and firm…fuck, he hadn't even kissed her yet. That was going to change. Today. Today, he'd taste her.

Taste…and touch. The silken skin at her throat and the slight swell of her breasts at the neckline of the dress, before the red fabric hid the rest. That perfect dress…demure and kind of old-fashioned, covering everything from her shoulders to just past her knees, but hinting at curves he couldn't wait to see, to touch, to stroke and hear her cries of pleasure as he…fuck.

She'd worn the red heels. The red Cinderella heels from the day they met. The ones he'd dreamed about every night since. Just him and her and those…

"Jason? Are you all right?"

He shook himself. "Yeah. Fine. It's normal for a guy to have porn-quality fantasies about his bride on their wedding day. Especially with you looking so fucking beautiful in that dress." He wanted to ask about the underwear she had on, but her rosy blush stopped him. He could imagine it for now, and see if the fantasy lived up to reality later. He'd savour every moment, too.

"Thank you," she mumbled.

They stood there awkwardly for a long moment before Jason's brain booted up and he said, "Um, the helicopter. Chariot. Whatever. Anyway, it's waiting on the helipad for us. Apparently it's all dolled up in wedding bows and stuff, so everyone at the hotel and the pearl farm knows we're getting married today, but they swear no one's told the press. We better get going before that changes."

Phuong paled. "Yes." She hurried off. Jason found he had to jog to keep up.

"There's the blushing bride," the pilot shouted as he came into view. He burst out laughing. "You're gunning for the headlines in that dress. I can see it now: 'Rock Star Marries Asian Mail-Order Bride'."

Phuong stopped dead. "What…what do you mean?" She stared at her skirt.

"Red dress, covered in envelopes?" Shou snorted.

"I didn't…didn't think…" Phuong's hands flapped in panic, like she was trying to hide as much of her dress as possible. "I have to get changed!" She darted away, but Jason stood squarely in her way, blocking the helipad gates.

Jason addressed the pilot: "There aren't going to be any headlines, right, mate? The resort's privacy policy means no press." After Shou's nod, Jason placed his hands on Phuong's shoulders. "Baby, I love you in this dress. Please don't change."

Her tensed-up shoulders, braced hard enough to charge down a football pitch, dropped as she exhaled so rapidly it looked like she'd been punched in the guts. Fearful eyes regarded him.

"If you say so," she said colourlessly, then turned and climbed into the helicopter.

Fuck. What had he said wrong this time?

FORTY-THREE

Shou landed the helicopter on a grassed oval, the goalposts at either end marking it as the local football field.

"The church is over there." He pointed at a clump of trees, through which Phuong could just see a cross poking out the top. "I'll wait here until you're done."

"No, you won't," Jason said. "We need witnesses. You're one of them."

Shou gave an exaggerated sigh as he jumped out of the cockpit. He threw open Phuong's door, bent in a deep bow and offered her his hand. "Anything I can do for the lovely lady."

Jason rolled his eyes, but Phuong smiled, resting her fingers lightly on Shou's palm as she stepped onto the grass. She smoothed her skirt, maybe taking a few more strokes than necessary, but she was too nervous to stop. If she could only stop her hands from shaking.

Jason slipped an arm around her shoulders and gave her a gentle squeeze. Somehow, his light touch had uncorked a bottle of champagne in her blood, making her lightheaded. She needed Jason's supportive arm to walk the hundred metres to the church, where they were met by a middle-aged man in priests' robes and a younger, similarly dressed man that he introduced as a seminarian, a student priest.

Phuong found her hand gripped in a surprisingly firm handshake from the priest, before Jason received the same treatment.

"Shall we?" the priest said, leading the way into the church.

She stepped inside the old-fashioned, white building and gasped. Instead of the dark interior she expected, it glowed in colours that brought the Kimberley environment inside. Terracotta tiles and red-brown timber pews formed the foundation underpinning the walls of beach-sand cream and shallow-sea aquamarine, but everything she saw was only the background setting for the most prominent feature of the church: everything was decorated in glittering shells. The tiles were edged with shells. The windows and all the pictures were framed in shells. The microphone podium was decorated with a religious design made out of shells. And the altar…well, all three altars, if you included the main one and the two smaller ones on either side of it…were inlaid with hundreds of oyster shells, each one as big as her head, the nacre catching the light and throwing it back in coruscating rainbows across each pearly surface.

"So beautiful," she breathed.

Jason's hands pressed on either side of her waist. "Not as beautiful as you look today."

She could feel the heat of his body, standing close behind her for just a moment before it was gone as he stepped up to the table in front of the altar. "Let's get started," he told the priest.

The priest coughed. "I understand you want simple, traditional vows and a short ceremony, but I want to warn you. Marriage isn't meant to be simple or short. It's a lifetime commitment from both of you, giving each other your love and loyalty, through whatever your lives may hold. It isn't something to enter into lightly. You do understand the depth of the commitment you're making today, don't you?" His eyes pierced Phuong's soul first.

Phuong nodded: she understood. Jason already had her loyalty. Everything she'd done to be here today was for him. Her love? He'd said he loved her, in his casual comment on the helipad that morning. Could she do any less?

Jason must have passed the priest's test, because the priest raised his voice like he was addressing an entire congregation instead of just the four of them: Jason, herself, the pilot and the priest-in-training.

"We are gathered here today to celebrate and witness the marriage of Phuong Tran and Jason Felix. Phuong and Jason, please join hands."

Jason turned to face her and enveloped her hands in his. Now she had eyes for no one but Jason. His honey-brown eyes held her in place as they warmed her heart. He loved her.

"Jason, do you take Phuong to be your wife, to have and to hold, for better or worse, for richer or poorer, in sickness and in health, to love and to cherish, from this day forward until death do you part?"

Jason squeezed her hands as he replied, "I do."

"Phuong, do you take Jason to be your husband…"

Husband. This man would be hers and hers alone, and she'd be his.

"…for better or worse…"

She could endure anything with him at her side. The very thought of him had helped her break free from Norman.

"…for richer or poorer…"

She wasn't marrying him for his money. He'd bought her too much already. Nothing mattered but him.

"…to love and to cherish…"

Could she love him? For all her business ideals, wanting a marriage to build her future, love had never been a part of her plan. But neither had a man like Jason. She would cherish him – she did already. But could she love him?

"…until death do you part?"

Did she love him?

Phuong wet her lips. "I…I do."

Jason's smile widened and for a moment the world stood still. There was no one but the two of them. Everything was perfect.

The priest cleared his throat. "Ah, the rings?"

The moment ended. "Right." Jason fished in his pocket for the boxes they'd bought from the jeweller yesterday. He flipped them open and dropped both rings onto his palm.

The priest nodded. He held his hand over Jason's and muttered a few words before drawing a cross in the air above the rings. "Now, give Phuong her ring and repeat after me, Jason…"

Phuong didn't hear the priest any more. All she heard

was Jason's voice telling her, "With this ring, I join my life with yours," as he slipped the enormous, golden diamond onto her finger.

She knew what she had to do. The gold band that remained, studded with smaller, but equally tawny diamonds, felt so heavy in her fingers, as if it held all the pain of her past. She drew in a deep, shaky breath. "With this ring, I join my life with yours." It slid easily onto his finger like it belonged there. She held his hand and the ring, and it felt like a weight had been lifted from her, buoyed by the joy their future held.

Please, let it hold joy and not too much pain, she begged the universe.

"By the exchange of vows and rings in front of these witnesses, you have declared your love and commitment to each other. I now pronounce you husband and wife." The priest produced a wry smile. "Now you may kiss the bride."

How had she forgotten this was coming? Their first kiss, in a church, in front of strangers and…

Jason's hand caressed her cheek, settling along the side of her face as his thumb grazed her lips. His other arm slipped around her waist, pulling her close.

Kiss him. Just kiss him!

Her lips parted, but she couldn't seem to draw any air in. Jason's face loomed closer, his eyes gentle and loving and…

His lips made contact.

The world went away.

A light brush at first, soft as a feather, followed by the firm press of his mouth on hers. She inhaled the sweet, sharp mint on his breath – her lungs worked once more – and she needed to taste. Her tongue darted out, caressing his lower lip, his shaven cheeks smooth under her fingers.

His breath stole inside her like pure oxygen, revivifying her as she welcomed him in. Her throat warmed and hummed in approval while her heart swelled, beating faster as it craved more of this delicious man, pumping a steady stream of life-giving bubbles through her blood until she felt filled with shaken-up champagne.

She barely felt when he broke their kiss, because her blood was still fizzing, the froth overflowing into her dazzled brain. "Oh, Jason," she whispered, embracing him.

"I'm all yours, baby," came the reply, rumbling through his chest as his arms enveloped her in safety, welcoming her home.

FORTY-FOUR

The moment Jason's lips touched Phuong's, everything changed. She relaxed, she responded, and the slow rumba of their tongues dancing together for the first time was music to his…well, everything really. Not just his cock, though that, too, of course. He'd be lying if he said that first, hot kiss hadn't made him think of sex.

The only reason he stopped kissing his beautiful wife was because the priest's loud, incessant throat-clearing got on his nerves.

"This is a church, Mr Felix. You're not officially married until you both sign the forms and the witnesses do, too."

Like that would stop them. Jason stroked her tongue one last time, promising more, before they reluctantly ascended the dais to deal with the priest's paperwork.

Jason didn't let go of Phuong the whole time, and he didn't intend to, either.

He waited until both the student priest and the pilot had signed the marriage certificate before he asked, "Are we done here?"

The priest nodded. Jason handed him the envelope containing the priest's payment and a hefty sweetener. The man took it and tucked it inside his robe, without even looking at the contents.

Shou remarked, "I better get you lovebirds back to your nest before you start doing things that'll get you thrown out of this church for indecency, right, Father?"

The priest smiled, but the only thing he said was, "Congratulations," before bidding them goodbye.

Jason and Phuong managed to restrain themselves until they were seated in the relative privacy of the helicopter, but the moment she turned to him with those pleading eyes and said, "Jason, would you kiss me —" all bets were off. The dance began again. He pulled her into his lap, wanting to feel her body pressed close to him because that's where it belonged.

"All right, you two. Rules of the helicopter say no sex in the back seat."

Jason dragged his lips from Phuong's so he could glare at the pilot. "Since when?"

"Since it's not safe. Buckle up, boys and girls, and I'll take you to where you can get a room." Shou grinned as he slammed the door.

Jason turned to Phuong. "Don't worry, baby. It's just a short flight, and I'll be all yours again."

But the passionate girl he'd been kissing only moments before had now turned ashen, sitting stiffly in her seat with her seatbelt cinched tight across her waist. She nodded, but her eyes never left the view out of the front windscreen.

What the fuck did he do wrong this time?

The rotors soon drowned out all other sound and, while he put his headphones on, Phuong's hung limply by her side. She wouldn't hear a word he or Shou said.

He must really have fucked up royally. Phuong left him wondering all the way back to the resort, where she jumped out of the helicopter before the blades had even stopped spinning. She set off down the path to the hotel instead of the villas.

He followed her, determined to get answers. "Where are you going?" he called, praying that she wouldn't leave.

"To my room to get my things," she tossed back, not slowing.

"Why?" His voice came out weaker than he wanted, but for once, he didn't care. She was his wife. They were supposed to be happy, not splitting up mere moments into their marriage.

She stopped, turned and stared. "Because...I thought because we're married now, you'd want me to live in your house instead of here. I packed my things before we left, but my bag is still in my hotel room." She paled even more. "Unless you don't want me to live in your house?"

Jason couldn't help it: he burst out laughing. "I thought you meant you were leaving. Of course you're moving in with me. I'm not going to make my wife walk across the whole damn island every time she wants my specialist services." He winked.

This didn't help as much as he'd hoped. If anything, it made her more flustered.

Jason went on, "And I won't let you carry anything

heavy, either. That's why the resort has a porter. We'll go to Reception and have someone bring your things over later."

Phuong lowered her eyes and nodded. Where was the passionate woman he'd kissed less than an hour before? There was no sign of any passion now. Instead, she was submissive. Sad. Resigned.

He stayed by her side until they reached the foyer, when he opened the door and ushered her through. He wasn't prepared for the chorus of clapping that greeted them, or the enormous bunch of flowers the hotel manager forced into Phuong's arms.

"Congratulations," Xan said, throwing a glance at Jason but keeping most of her attention on Phuong. She tapped Phuong's ID wristband. "This'll now give you access to Jay's villa, as well as all the normal guest facilities on the island. Tap three times to trigger the locks if you don't want to be disturbed."

A wave of laughter swept around the room. It looked like most of the hotel staff had assembled to offer their congratulations. So much for a secret wedding.

But these were his staff and the people he lived with. If he'd gotten married while on tour, the roadies might have done the same thing. Yeah, there'd have been more beer and bourbon, and fewer flowers, but the intent would have been the same. Weddings were a time to celebrate.

Jason forced his frown into a stage smile as he curled a supportive arm around Phuong. "Thank you. We're trying to keep it a secret from the press for just a bit longer, and I hope you're all willing to help. We'll announce it to the public in a week or two, but, right now, we're just going to take the time to enjoy our honeymoon." He grinned and winked just like he used to do for the fangirls when he stood on stage, the rock idol of millions. Now, he couldn't even keep his own wife happy.

He was tired of performing, so he cut the show short. "You know what? Can someone bring her bags from her room to the villa? I think my beautiful bride and I need some alone time. What better place to start the honeymoon early than Romance Island Resort?" Jason grabbed her hand and towed her outside. She followed him along the path that skirted the lagoon. The laughter and bawdy catcalls faded as they rounded the bend. Okay, maybe they weren't all that different to roadies, after all.

When they reached Villa Penguin, Jay waved his wrist at the scanner. Before Phuong could step inside, he scooped her up and carried her across the threshold, then set her down on the tiles. Some Prince Charming he was – he should have carried her all the way to the house, not just a few steps. Another fuck-up he hoped she'd forgive him for.

He pointed as he strode through the house. "That's the bathroom, kitchen, lounge, my bedroom…and that's the guest room. I asked Reception to make the guest room romantic and stuff, so I hope they did okay." He peered in. Little flickering lights sat on all the surfaces – battery powered, seeing as fire hazards like candles weren't allowed at the hotel – except for the bed, which had a huge heart made out of frangipanis on top of the bedspread. In the middle sat a heart-shaped box that contained what the resort called its honeymoon pack: enough condoms to last any normal couple for a month, and enough lube to slide an elephant into a beer bottle. "Want to see if it works?"

"If what works?" Fear had returned to her face, with its

evil sidekick, panic.

The romantic atmosphere, Jason wanted to say, but there was no point. It was as fucked as he was.

The door chimed to announce the porter's arrival, saving Jason from having to answer. He seized the bag, called his thanks over his shoulder before the door slid shut, and carried it to Phuong.

"Where do you want this? My room, or the guest room?"

Phuong looked lost. "Here, I guess, if this is where you want to...where we'll..." She blushed.

Too late, Jason remembered how much she didn't like talking about sex. He had to change the subject, but he couldn't think of anything but sex. Fuck! He dropped the bag on the floor. "Do you want to try the bed out now, or order an early dinner first?" he hazarded, looking longingly at the bed.

"Dinner, please," Phuong replied promptly. "I've been too nervous to eat much all day."

A decent meal would give them both the stamina to go all night. Jason couldn't argue with that.

"Right. Room service menu's in the kitchen. Let's get the chefs to prepare something special for us tonight. Pick your pleasure, baby. I'll make it happen."

He would, too.

FORTY-FIVE

Phuong toyed with her food, hoping Jay didn't notice how little she'd eaten. If they'd had the lobster she'd originally ordered, maybe she'd have eaten more, but they were all out of lobster, crabs and anything that wasn't prawns, so an unappetising shrimp salad had arrived instead. She'd managed to choke down a few bites before she'd remembered what would follow dinner. That almost made her bring it all back up again. Better not to eat anything else than to embarrass herself in front of Jason on their first night together. She'd soon be embarrassed enough without throwing nausea into the mix.

Jason didn't seem to be nervous at all. He wolfed down his steak and all that went with it, but he managed to do it without dribbling food down his front, like Norman might have. He didn't talk with his mouth full, either, but he didn't say much during the meal. He'd paused several times to smile at her across the table, something Norman had never done.

He wasn't Norman. Jason was a much better man in every way. That's why she could do this. She would do this. For him. Because she loved him and he wanted this.

"Are you ready for dessert?" Jason asked eagerly, wiping all the traces of food off his face with the napkin. Not that there'd been much to start with. "Or do you want to put your new stallion through his paces, make me show you what I can do, and dessert can wait for intermission?" He winked.

Her heart sank. Her time was up. Time to get it over with.

"I just need to use the bathroom. Give me a few minutes to get ready. I'll meet you in the bedroom," Phuong managed to say with what she hoped was a smile. She shoved back from the table, her chair screeching as it scraped across the tiles. The noise was nothing compared to the building scream in her own head. She fled for the sanctuary of the bathroom and locked the door.

She sank to the floor, shaking. She should've told Jason she had no idea what she was doing when it came to sex. Yes, this bit went there, but…aside from grunting and the mess at the end, she was less experienced than she let on. No man had ever seen her naked except Norman, and he was the only man she'd ever slept with. His expert opinion, based on more experience than she'd ever had, was that she was useless in bed, so she should lie back, take what she was given and thank him at the end.

What would Jason say when he found out? If anything, Jason had been with more girls than Norman and probably better girls, too. Ones who could do anything he asked, and all night, too. Not a nervous wreck who'd never…

Jason knocked on the bathroom door. "You all right in there, baby? I want a few minutes in there after you're done. I need to get ready, too."

Phuong shot to her feet. "Sure," she said breathlessly, slipping out the door and past him before she lost her nerve.

When the bathroom door closed behind Jason, she bolted for the bedroom. The box, the flowers…she swept them onto the bedside table, leaving the white bedspread to gape at her blankly as she stripped off her clothes. Norman had torn far too many things in his eagerness to undress her, and Jason was so much stronger. She didn't want to take the risk with her lovely wedding dress. She threw her underwear on the chair and draped the dress over the top.

She surveyed her naked body. She was too thin, but there was nothing she could do about that now. Even the thought of food made her ill. Maybe tomorrow she'd have her appetite back when this ordeal was over. Or at least less of an ordeal, because she'd know what he liked. Maybe.

She stretched out on the bed, like Norman had insisted all his ladies did. Lie and wait, legs spread, a smile pasted on her face because he'd called her ungrateful and all sorts of other things if she frowned during his nightly groping and grunting sessions. Frigid, ungrateful, uppity, uptight, juiceless, rhymed with useless and she was…

Tears built and threatened to escape, but Phuong blinked furiously. She couldn't cry. Crying meant she was disappointed in him and she wasn't, she wasn't…Norman was all she'd ever known and she couldn't be disappointed if she didn't know any better.

Jason would be better. He had to be. And maybe, if she asked carefully, he'd be willing to help her learn to be better…but only if she could satisfy him tonight.

Open legs, closed eyes: please, let her satisfy him tonight.

"Wow, baby, if I'd known you were that eager, I'd have come faster. I figured we'd take our time, but I'm not going to argue."

Phuong cracked one eye open. Jason stood in the doorway, unbuttoning his shirt as he surveyed her body. He didn't frown or look disgusted – that was a start.

"Hurry," she begged, feeling her self-control slipping. Her heart galloped in her chest and her breathing quickened. She'd scream, she'd run and hide and never, ever come back. She didn't want to do this, didn't want, didn't want, didn't…

"Sure, baby."

Phuong felt the mattress sink under his weight. His lips lightly brushed hers as his hand skimmed down her throat, her chest, her belly and down her leg, then crept up her inner thigh. Her breath caught in her throat as he pierced her with one thick finger.

"You're not ready for me, baby." The finger withdrew.

"Yes, I am!" she insisted, clenching her hands into fists. "Now, take me now!" Or never.

Jason sighed. "You're lying. You don't want me at all. You're not even wet, baby." The bed shifted as he moved away from her. "I only sleep with willing girls, Phuong. I thought today in the church that I was wrong, that maybe you were…I mean, you married me, for fuck's sake!

Wishful thinking, I guess." He sighed again. "Well, good night." A moment later, she heard the sound of a door closing.

What? Phuong jumped up, scissoring her legs shut and dragging the bedspread with her. Jason was gone — into his bedroom, behind a closed door. He'd rejected her utterly.

Norman was right: she was useless.

And now Jason knew it, too.

FORTY-SIX

So much for the fucking honeymoon. It had been a week. Phuong still wouldn't meet his eyes. He'd tried a thousand times to talk to her, but the words died before they left his mouth. He'd slept with heaps of girls before her, but every single damn one was willing. If they said no, fine. Plenty more where they came from. Even the ones who said no and meant yes…usually he left those alone, too. Audra had been the exception and look where that had gotten him.

But what the fuck did you do with a girl whose body and soul screamed NO while her lips lied and begged for something she didn't want?

Stay the fuck away, was his first thought. He didn't need crazy girls in his life. Crazy fangirls, yes, but not in his bed or his house.

But she was his wife. What did you do when your wife didn't want you and all she did was lie to you?

Divorce, like his parents had? Fuck that. His mum should never have married his dad, and she'd never wanted him, so he and his dad had been better off alone. Leslie wasn't even Mum in his mind; never had been. But then Dad had met Jo's mum and didn't her bastard of a boyfriend just beat all…so they married. Miriam became Mum, and Jo got to share his dad, too. Happy endings. That's what life was about. Not this fucked-up shit.

He glanced at the stranger in his kitchen: Phuong with her downcast eyes, shoulders hunched like she was warding off a blow. As if he'd hit her or do anything to hurt her.

The urge rose up again. That one, where he wanted to take her in his arms and protect her, but he couldn't. He had to protect her from herself, which meant him, too. Or she'd beg him for sex like she had on their wedding night, when she wanted nothing of the sort.

What kind of girl did that?

"What are you doing today?" he fired off.

She shuddered as if his words had actually hit her. "I don't know." That colourless tone squeezed his heart. "Maybe when I'm finished here, I'll clean the bathroom again. I found some bleach under the sink that might get that rust out of the grout in the shower."

She'd…what?

"Why would you want to clean the bathroom? That's the maid's job, not yours." Jason stared at her and realised what she was doing. "Why are you washing dishes? We have a dishwasher!"

"I tried to cook something last night, but I burned it and now it's stuck to the pan. I don't know if the dishwasher can get it off, but I've been scrubbing it for half an hour now and, look, it's coming clean." She held out the dripping casserole dish like an offering to a vengeful deity.

What kind of girl…

"Phuong, don't clean stuff. And you don't need to cook – whatever you want, just order it from Catering. The chefs will make it for you. They'll deliver it to your door. You live in a resort in paradise with staff. Do what you want to do. Go to the gym, book a session with the personal trainer, play a round of pool or tennis or volleyball. Get a book from the library and read it on the beach. Go for a walk on one of the beaches that you'll have all to yourself. Swim in the lagoon and meet the fish. Go catch a fish and get the chefs to prepare it for you however you like. Do something that makes you happy. What do you want to do?"

She swallowed painfully. "Maybe…I could go to the resort library and see if I can borrow a book." She made it sound like a visit to the dreaded dentist.

He nodded. "You do that." And he'd avoid the library so he wouldn't have to see her and know how badly he'd fucked up. A happy wife? Try a miserable one. So much for being a rock star that every woman wanted. Now his own wife hated him.

The phone shrilled, dragging him out of his depressing thoughts. "Yeah?" he answered.

"Normal people say hello. Hello, Jason," Jo snapped.

"Hi, sis." Jo understood women. She was one, after all. Maybe she could help. Jason glanced at Phuong and headed out the door so he could talk in private. "How's the corporate world this week?"

He half-listened to her drone on about quarterly reports, EBITDA and some bloke named Bas until he reached the end of the jetty, when he interrupted with, "Jo? What should I do when a girl acts like she's not that into me, but she lies about stuff and when we kissed, it was all fireworks and shit, and I'd give anything to be able to protect her, but now…"

"Are you talking about Angel? If this is about Angel, you stay the hell away from her, Jason. I mean it. After what you did to her, she has every right to be angry. If I were her, I'd have kicked your arse into next week with steel-capped boots."

"No! This isn't about her at all. I just…" Fucked up again. "What do you do to get, you know, in the mood?"

"Jason, tell me you didn't just ask me about my foreplay preferences. You're my brother. You absolutely do NOT need to know that."

Fine. Foreplay. He could Google that shit. "What are you calling for, anyway?"

Jo made an impatient noise. "The new business plan for the resort. After Meier, your new manager is amazing. The plans she has for the place. Most of the things she wants to change won't require much capital, though she will need a few extra FTE, but in the high season, I think you might be able to manage with short-term contracts. But the projections…"

"What the fuck are you on about?" Jason growled. "What business plan?"

"Haven't you been reading your emails? She sent it a week ago."

When he fucked up with Phuong. "I've been busy."

"Whatever her name is, pull your bits out of her and put your business pants on. This is important. It's about the future of your business. Our business, in case I need to remind you. Now, Xan's arranged a meeting for Monday to discuss the half-yearly reports and the new plan. I want you to be there. No excuses. And read the damn plan in the meantime!" She ended the call without another word.

Jason contemplated calling her back. Next, he considered throwing the fucking phone into the ocean because there was no one he could call to fix this. Adding insult to injury, the hotel's new manager, his fucking employee, was going to make changes to his resort without his permission. Well, fuck that. He might not be able to fix his marriage, but his manager? Time to put that bitch in her place.

He marched up to the main building, taking the public path this time because he wanted her to see him coming. She'd closed her office door, but that wouldn't keep him out. Jason wrenched it open and stormed in, only to find her office empty.

"Where's the manager?" he demanded of the bloke at the reception desk.

"It's her day off, so I dunno. Have you tried her house?"

Living on an island was awesome. He thanked the bloke and strode through the staff accommodation to the manager's house. No rum on her veranda this time. Just a hot chick in a bikini, who…fuck.

"Is the honeymoon over, then?" Xan asked, adjusting her bikini top. "I wondered how long it'd take before you became bored with that sweet girl." She glanced at his groin. "Oh, no. No. That's wrong on all sorts of levels. You don't cheat on your wife on your honeymoon. Even that's low for you. Or is she just not doing it for you?"

"My wife is none of your fucking business." Jason tried to hide his hard-on behind his hands, hoping it would go away. He didn't like this woman, let alone want to touch her. "Put some clothes on, will you? I came to talk business. About the meeting on Monday. How come the first I hear about your business plan is a phone call from my sister?"

Xan shrugged. "I emailed it to you both at the same time. I didn't expect you to look at it before Monday, when I can talk you through it. I'm not about to explain it to you now. Honestly, I didn't plan on discussing it for another week at least, but Jo called yesterday. She's so eager to start on some of it that I agreed to move the meeting up to Monday. We can discuss it then, but not today. It's my day off. I'm going to explore the lagoon. You're on your honeymoon. You should be playing hide the sausage with your wife. She'll probably enjoy the respite on Monday, or are you going to slip off during a coffee break for a quickie?"

Jason's heart sank like a stone. "Did you tell Jo about my wife?"

"Of course not. Why on Earth would we talk about you?"

If Jo knew how badly he'd messed up his marriage, he'd never hear the end of it. "You can't tell her. Not now, and not on Monday. She's not to know about Phuong, or the wedding at all."

Xan dropped her flippers. "You haven't told your family you're married?" Jason didn't like the gleam in her eye. "Now, why wouldn't you do that? Is it because they won't approve of her? You're ashamed of her, aren't you? Go on, admit it. You're ashamed of your wife!"

"All right, I admit it! I'm ashamed!" Jason shouted, scaring something into flight in the nearby bushes. Rats, probably, seeing as no birds rose above the jungle canopy. He lowered his voice so the whole staff compound couldn't hear him. "Not ashamed of her. Ashamed of me. Ashamed because I've been married a week and my wife hates me so much she doesn't want me to touch her." He waved at the tent he'd pitched in his pants. "So I'm fucking frustrated, yeah, because I'm not used to going without. So even you in your skimpy…swim gear gets me going. Don't take it as a compliment. I'd fuck almost anything in a skirt right now and I wouldn't fuck you." He glared at her. He meant it, too. The manager's tits were way bigger than he wanted in his women. Phuong's, however… "I'll take whatever I can get from my unwilling wife over anything from you." He set off down the jungle path back to Villa Penguin.

"You know marital rape's a crime in Australia!" Xan called after him. "If you hurt that girl, you'll have hell to pay. Your rock star reputation won't protect you if the police get a hold of you. You'll be going to prison like all the other pricks. And then you'll really discover what rape's like…"

Jason stopped dead. That was it. Jo and Xan had both recognised it, but he hadn't. Phuong acted just like Angel had after…all that happened to her. No wonder his every instinct told him to protect her and not to touch her. He hadn't messed up his marriage completely yet. But he knew how to make it right.

FORTY-SEVEN

Phuong waited until Jason was well down the path to the hotel before she ducked into the jungle track that led through the staff accommodation to the library. It was like the servants' entrance to the villas and it suited her, she thought. Just as long as none of the real staff saw her and told her off for using their secret track.

When she stepped out of the jungle behind the last house, she heard voices, so she cautiously crept to the corner and peered around.

She heard Jason's voice clearly: "You can't tell her. Not now, and not on Monday. She's not to know about Phuong, or the wedding at all."

The feminine voice that followed was harder to hear, but it rose in volume until she could make out the words. What she did hear froze her heart.

"You're ashamed of her, aren't you? Go on, admit it.

You're ashamed of your wife!" the English manager hissed.

"All right, I admit it! I'm ashamed!" Jason shouted back.

Phuong didn't wait to hear any more. Instead, she did what she did best: she bolted.

By the time she reached the villa, she was so blinded by tears that she couldn't see the scanner. It took a few wild swipes before the door swished open to grant her sanctuary.

Not much, though. Jason's words still rang through her head, taunting her. Of course he was ashamed of her. She was a useless wife. She couldn't cook, he didn't need her to clean and as for sex…he hadn't touched her since their aborted wedding night. Wouldn't even look at her. Some wife she was, when her own husband didn't want her.

She'd clean the bathroom with bleach, like she'd originally planned, she decided. Grout should be white, not red like the road on the mainland. She spritzed the tiles with the spray bottle and set to scrubbing. The stench of bleach seared her nostrils, tasting like citrus in the back of her throat, but she found it soothing. The bathroom had been the only place she could get away from Norman – especially when it smelled of cleaning chemicals. And if it made things better with Jason, all the better.

"Phuong? Baby?" Jason stood in the doorway, one arm over his face to block out the fumes. "What are you doing in here?" He strode across the room and shoved the window wide, then waved the outside door open. He jammed the rubbish bin between the door and the wall to keep it from closing. The exhaust fan clicked on and whirred overhead. "Can I talk to you for a minute? Please?" He paused, then added, "In the other room. This one reeks."

"But I need to finish – " she began, waving at the shower with her scrubbing brush.

"Baby, I've already told you that you don't need to clean anything in this house. Why do you think you need to scrub the floor?"

She stared at him for a long time, not knowing what to say. Nothing seemed right. Finally, she said, "I'm trying to be a good wife the only way I know how. I can't cook, and you've made it perfectly clear that you're not interested in sex, so cleaning…cleaning is all I can do." She wouldn't mention the conversation she'd overheard. She had a tiny speck of pride left, after all, and she'd lose that if she admitted to accidental eavesdropping.

"Who told you I'm not interested in sex? Do I look like a fucking monk? A sex maniac, maybe, but not so crazy I can't see what's going on. You meant that kiss in the church, didn't you? With every fucking fibre of your being?"

Now he wanted her to lay her feelings out in the open, so he could smash them like he'd done to her heart on their wedding night? No way would she admit she loved him when he had no feelings for her.

He crouched down so he was on the same level as her. "Look me in the eye and tell me, Phuong. Do you want me to kiss you like we did then?"

"Yes." Her response slipped out before she could stop it.

"Right now?"

Phuong stared at his outstretched hand. YES. She ripped off her gloves, seized his hand and let him help her to her feet and into his arms, where she belonged. Phuong savoured the safety for a moment before tilting her head so she could stare into his eyes. Warm honey and everything she wanted, so she stretched up to marry her mouth with his once more. Marital bliss in a single, passionate kiss.

When she rested her head against his chest once more, gasping for breath, she heard his pounding heart – she wasn't the only one enjoying herself.

"I have a million more where that came from, baby. All for you."

Phuong smiled and said nothing, because nothing needed to be said.

"And what if I offered you a night of bliss, better than anything you ever had, full of sex better than you've ever dreamed of?"

Her heart froze and her limbs turned leaden, sending clanging alarm bells through her head. She tried to pull away, but –

"It's all right, baby. You don't need to answer that. I already know."

Another kiss calmed her; a third sent her heart racing and a fourth ended too soon.

When she met his eyes once more to ask why, she saw sadness.

"Who hurt you, baby? Who made you hate sex so much?"

He knew about Norman.

Phuong wrenched free of his grasp. She eyed the open door, knowing she could be through it and off at a run before he could stop her, but it didn't matter. He'd catch up and keep pace with her, just like he did last time. She'd still have to answer.

She swallowed several times, but the lump in her throat

wouldn't leave. "I can't tell you. I can't. I just…can't."

"Did you tell the police? If someone attacked you and hurt you, you have to report it. Rapists shouldn't be allowed to go unpunished. He'll do it again. He must be stopped."

She stared at him. "Rape? No, it wasn't like that."

"Then tell me what happened, baby. Tell me his name."

No. He could never know about Norman. "No, I can't. It's not what you think. I'm not a rape victim." No, she'd walked into the relationship with her eyes open. Every time she'd opened her legs for that bastard, it had been her choice. The price of the future, or so she'd thought. How could she tell Jason that? He'd never understand.

Jason nodded slowly. "Right. Okay. Not rape. Maybe he convinced you to have sex when you didn't want to. Do things you didn't want to. Did he hurt you, baby?"

Shakily, she nodded. "But he didn't know. I didn't tell him after the first time because he said if it hurt after the first time, then there must be something wrong with me and even though I never liked it, I didn't…didn't want…" This time, she couldn't stop the tears from coming.

"Tell me his name, baby. That fucker should die for hurting you."

She stared at him, even as more tears blurred her vision. "You can't kill him, Jason. You can't!"

"Oh, not me. I know people, that's all. People who hate rapists even more than I do. People who'll pay him a visit and make him just disappear, so he'll never, ever bother you again." He looked like he meant it, too.

"He won't. He'll never find me. I'm safe now with you." The tighter she held Jason, the more she believed it. Had to believe it.

Gently, he stroked her hair. "You sure are, baby. I swear I'll never let anyone hurt you. Especially not me. And this sex thing?" He cupped her chin and stared into her eyes. "We'll work it out. When you're ready for me to do things to your body that'll blow your mind, you tell me, and we'll take it slow. But not until you're ready."

Privately, Phuong thought she soon would be. If he asked her now, she'd say yes. But she didn't tell him yet. For the moment, she just wanted to stay secure in his arms.

FORTY-EIGHT

The next day, four hundred and eighty-three kisses later — not that he was counting or anything — Jason reluctantly left Phuong watching TV so he could look through the email Xan had sent, detailing her plans for his resort. Bad news first — he clicked on the half-yearly financial report, knowing it couldn't be good.

Columns of numbers filled his laptop screen in endless ranks of red and black. Meier used to explain it all to him, but he didn't think Xan would be quite as accommodating. No, he had to wrap his head around these figures before their meeting on Monday so he wouldn't look like a complete fool.

But there were pages and pages of numbers. None of them meant anything to him. He should be sitting on the couch with Phuong, her body tucked against his, as he did his damnedest to get her to relax around him enough for him to show her how a honeymoon was supposed to work.

Instead, he was giving himself a headache. "Fuck," he swore softly.

She heard. "What is it?" Before he'd opened his mouth to respond, she crossed the room. Phuong leaned over his shoulder, peering at the fucking figures. "Oh, that's not good. No bar should stay in business with a loss like that. And the margin's increasing, too…when was it last in profit?" She reached over and tapped the touchpad, bring up another mess of columns. "Wow. Let's see if I can find your drain…ah, yep. Here. You're spending thousands a month on this product, but there don't seem to be any sales of it, yet the orders keep coming. Where else have you got a loss this big? I know I saw another one…oh, in staff meals. Well, that makes sense. I take it you're not charging staff for room and board, which is fair, but when you compare it to the number of staff at the resort, this is more than I paid for full room and board at the residential college I used to stay at. You're not putting your staff up in hotel rooms and feeding them exotic seafood every day, are you?"

Jason recovered from his surprise enough to manage a short laugh. "No. The food in the staff dining room's pretty basic, or so I've been told. They only get seafood if the chef's messed up, and it's not suitable to serve to guests in the public restaurant. As for the accommodation…mining camp dongas, and little ones at that." He stared at her. "How come you know so much about hotel running costs?"

Phuong shrugged, but she also smiled. "I'm in my final year of a business degree, with a double major in accounting. My father's company owns some small hotels in Vietnam and Singapore. He sent me to university here so I could learn to run his business. Occasionally, he'd ask me to check the financials when something didn't seem right…" She trailed off. "But that's all changed now. After Dad died, my brother took over the company with his wife's brother as Chief Financial Officer. The only numbers I'm likely to see from them now are if I get a job with whatever company handles receivership when those two bankrupt it."

Jason didn't understand. "Sorry about your dad, but why are you letting your brother destroy what he built? Sounds like your dad wanted to keep the company for you. He was training you to take over as his successor, not your brother. Why…?"

Phuong slid into the seat beside him. "It's a long story, but my brother's older than me. What my father didn't know is that he paid his way through business school by getting ghostwriters to write his assignments. He's also under his wife's thumb, and he believes everything his cheating, lying, thieving brother-in-law says, because they went to university together. They said my education was a drain on the company, with no hope of a return, so when my father died, Thuan stopped paying my tuition and board. But it wouldn't have helped – Felipe's running the company into the ground, or making it look that way, while he's building the money to buy it. Dad knew, but he couldn't prove it. He was waiting for me to be qualified so I could replace Felipe and find out what he'd done with the money. You can only trust family, he said. And I did, but my brother trusts his new family more than me, so there's nothing I can do now."

"You could finish your degree," Jason pointed out.

Phuong smiled again. "Yes, thanks to you, I can, but the

semester doesn't start for a few weeks and that will still take me a year. With no one to hide his dodgy dealings from, Felipe might destroy the company within that time. He might hire Thuan when he takes over, but he won't take me." She shrugged. "I have…new family now. Family I can trust and maybe help." She nodded at the laptop. "May I take a look?"

"Absolutely." Instead of sliding the laptop across the table to her, he pulled her into his lap. Now he could hold his wife in his arms and kiss everything he could reach, while she translated numbers into something he could understand. If he'd known he'd snag such a wonderful woman when he created a profile on the mail-order bride website, he would've done it sooner. As it was…he was just lucky.

More kisses. Four hundred and ninety-one, two, three… Jason slid a hand under the table and started stroking her leg through the silky material of her skirt.

She broke four hundred and ninety-four to lean forward, closer to the computer screen. "I think I need to see some earlier reports, ones from previous years. I can't be certain, but I think I've found your problem. It's specific products, and…you know, that feels really nice."

Jason grinned. "I can do better than nice. Here's the deal. I'll get you whatever figures you want tomorrow. You work your magic with them and tell me what they mean. Tonight…let me show you a bit of my sort of magic."

She stiffened. "You mean…sex?"

That one word…just three letters…the way she said it, like she was surprised. As if she wasn't sitting firmly on his hard-on, squirming as she considered the idea and teasing him like the minx she was.

Four hundred and ninety-five, then six and seven before he replied, "No. I said we'd take it slow. Call it…foreplay."

"Foreplay before…Jason, I'm scared."

Jason wasn't fazed. "A long time before. No need to be scared, baby. The pants aren't coming off tonight. Not mine, anyway. Your underwear…you should take that off first."

She didn't, though. Inwardly, Jason swore. He'd taken her too far, too fast and she was poised to run.

"One hand!" he blurted out. "I'll pleasure you with just one hand. Five fingers, all pleasure with no pain. I promise you'll want more. I want to give you this, baby. Please."

"Jason…" She twisted around for a tentative four-hundred and ninety-eight, before following it up with a far more confident nine. "Yes." Phuong wiggled out of her knickers and kicked them under the table.

Jason's hand crept under her skirt, caressing her skin. Closer and closer until with one light stroke he parted the lips of her pussy…her wet pussy, he was pleased to find, and felt her shiver as he touched her pearl. Yeah, chicks might call it a clitoris, but to him it would always be a pearl because of how it made girls glow when he did this right. And he always did this right.

"How's that feel, baby? Not hurting you, am I?" He drew a circle with his thumb, slow and firm.

"G-good," she breathed. "So good…oh!" She closed her eyes, letting her head fall back against his shoulder. He applied more pressure, and she let out a little whimper of delight, parting her thighs.

That was all the opening Jason needed. He uncurled one

finger and eased it inside her, followed by a second as she clenched around him, then relaxed again. He didn't stop circling – no, not when she was so close. Fuck, he couldn't take his eyes off her rapturous face.

"O-o-o-oh!" Part moan, part exclamation was the only way to describe the sound she made when he pushed her over the brink. A tear trickled down her cheek as she blinked at him, unseeing.

"Did you like that, baby?" he asked. "I have plenty more where that came from. A lifetime of orgasms, all with your name on them."

Phuong gasped for breath before she managed to say, "I'll take a dozen now and tomorrow –"

Jason burst out laughing. "Then I better get you to the bedroom, baby." First, he leaned down to kiss her one more time, knowing it wouldn't be kisses he'd be counting any more.

FORTY-NINE

On Monday morning, Phuong woke up in bed beside her husband, and she was happy. It probably had a lot to do with the husbandly hand stroking her thigh, coaxing her to open her legs so he could laugh at the faces she made when he sent her to her own personal nirvana. Oh, but he was amazing at that.

It took some time before she drifted down to Earth, where Jason was licking his fingers as he lay on the bed beside her, the image of the rock god he truly was. And rock hard, too, or he looked it. If it got any bigger, it wouldn't fit inside her, of that she was certain.

"You want my cock now, baby? Wondering what it'll feel like, buried deep inside you?" Warm honey laughing at her. He'd said the same thing last night, and the night before that, but when she admitted it, all he'd said was, "Soon."

This time, she tried a different tack. "Wondering what it feels like now."

"Wonder no more." He seized her hand in his and wrapped it around the shaft of his cock.

Soft and yet still hard. She stroked him a few times, feeling his pulse beating through hot skin.

"You'll need both hands for that, baby, but if you're offering, I'll lay back and let you do whatever you want with me." True to his word, Jason folded his arms behind his head, fixing his gaze on her.

"I don't know what I'm doing," she confessed. "I've never done this before."

Jason held up his curled hand and pumped it a few times. "Teenage boys can do it, and you're a dream by comparison. Whatever you want to give, baby, I'll take it."

"Teenage boys?" Norman had done things with boys in Thailand, he'd told her when he was particularly drunk one night. Not Jason, too!

"Yeah. I haven't been one for a while, but I wasn't always the irresistible man I am now. When I was at high school, it was jacking off myself or nothing." He stared at her. "What, you thought I'd let kids touch my dick? Fuck no! Just beautiful women like you, and now, only you." His hand wrapped around both of hers, guiding her up and down his length. Jason closed his eyes. "Fuck, it feels awesome when you do that. Just keep stroking. Just like that."

Somewhere in the house, a phone rang.

"Don't stop now. They can fucking wait." He raised his voice to shout, "Phuong's working her fucking magic right now, mate, so fuck off!"

She increased the pace and the pressure, like he'd done with her, and was rewarded with a groan. Maybe she wasn't so bad after all.

"Fuck, baby, if I'd known you were this good with your hands…oh fuuuuuck!"

Well, that was messy, Phuong reflected. She lifted a finger to her lips, giving the tip a tiny lick. Salty.

"You need a shower, baby."

She did. So did he.

He pulled her into the bathroom and into the shower cubicle with him, which was a tight fit. It wasn't until he reached for the soap that she realised they stood face to face, naked, for the first time, and she wasn't afraid any more.

"I made the mess. Let me clean it up," she offered, taking the soap from him. She worked it to a lather and applied the foam to his chest, stroking the stuff down his abs, tracing every muscle like she'd wanted to do since she first saw her name written across them. More soap, so she could do it again.

"You just going to wash my belly? My cock's plenty dirty, too. Not to mention the other muscles I kept in shape for you, baby." He dropped his voice lower. "Once you're finished with me, it'll be my turn to take care of you."

Yes! Not because she had to, but because she wanted to. Phuong stared down for a long, long time before she said, "If I told you I was ready for sex now, all of you and all of me, what would you say?"

Jason slid a hand under her chin and tilted until his eyes met hers. "I'd say that's fucking awesome, baby. Do you want to do it right here in the shower, or do you want the first time to be in the bed? There's the beach, too."

Phuong paled. "On a public beach? Oh, no. I couldn't do that."

"Don't knock it until you've tried it. Plus, we have a private beach here. I'll show you."

She laughed shakily. "All right. Let me get dressed first."

Phuong dressed in record time, but Jason still beat her, given all he donned was a pair of board shorts.

He shoved a handful of condoms into his pocket and winked. "I think you'll like it, and we won't want to stop to get more supplies," he said.

Someone started hammering on the front door.

"Fuck off!" Jason roared.

"I can override any lock you have on that door! You're already twenty minutes later for this meeting and we can't make any decisions without the primary shareholder!"

"We're busy!" he shouted back.

"You've got that poor girl in there with you? What have you done to her?"

The door whooshed open. A frantic Xan stood on the threshold, staring.

Phuong stared, too…at her feet.

"Nothing she didn't ask for, and she liked the lot," Jason said smugly. "Right, baby?"

Phuong nodded.

"Why didn't you answer the phone?" Xan persisted.

"We were busy. It's our fucking honeymoon. What do you think I was doing?" Jason stepped up to the door, so he stood toe to toe with the hotel manager. "Pleasing my wife, that's what. Let's get this meeting over with. Phuong and I have plans." He reached for her. "Coming, baby? You understand this stuff better than I do."

Leaving Xan standing speechless in their wake, Jason led the way along the path to the hotel.

FIFTY

Jo's face appeared on the projector screen on the meeting room wall. Xan breathed a sigh of relief. She'd never been that good at video calls, and the internet connection out here was patchy at best, especially in the wet season. Keeping her eyes on the screen stopped her from staring at the odd couple across the table, too – Jay Felix in nothing but a pair of low-slung board shorts, sitting beside the sweet girl he'd somehow bullied into becoming his wife. Why he wanted her in this meeting, she didn't know. Perhaps the girl would run away if he was out of sight.

Xan resolved to get the girl alone for a moment, to ask her if everything was all right.

"So, let's get the financials dealt with first," Jo said. "Jason, are you ready to sign off on the half-yearly report?"

"You mean the spreadsheets full of numbers? No," he replied.

"Xan already went over the numbers with me earlier. Everything seems in order, aside from the huge loss the hotel's running at, which brings us to her plans for recouping those losses – "

"I said no," Jason insisted, rising. "The report isn't in order. It's because Meier was ripping me off. Phuong found it – you tell them, baby."

To Xan's surprise, the girl cleared her throat. "He's right. Your biggest deficits are in staff catering and alcohol for the bar, followed by staff transport. I did a preliminary review of the figures Jason showed me, along with that of the last two years. It seems that there's been an increase in orders of certain luxury products that never appeared on the menu in the bar, restaurant or the staff dining room. For example, there's a brand of rum the bar doesn't carry, yet a large order arrives every month. It has for many years now. Then there's the alcohol in the staff catering order – alcohol that the staff never see, as it's not part of their menu, either. This is the opposite to the stuff for the bar – judging by the orders, they're extremely low price products. Cheap beer and spirits, cask wine…in huge quantities. These date back to when Mr Felix first purchased the resort, and he assures me he hasn't been drinking them. He can't have – unless he was permanently drunk for that whole time."

Xan stared pointedly at Jay. Lying to his little wife about his drinking. Oh, that was low. When she took the girl aside, she should also mention his alcohol problem.

"The orders match a rise in staff transport costs – both helicopters and vehicles. As there aren't any vehicles here on the island, I assume they're on the mainland? Perhaps based at the pearl farm, or in town?"

Xan nodded. "We try to keep two four-wheel drives at the farm, though sometimes one gets stuck in town when the road's closed. Then, it gets parked at the airport."

"Every trip gets logged with a purpose. Meetings, staff interviews, etcetera, so it can be allocated to an expense category. There's some sort of approval required for those, right?"

Once again, Xan nodded. "I sign half a dozen of them every week. Usually carrier boat trips to the mainland, or use of a car to drive into town when they're on leave. Oh, and charter flights. Planes, not helicopters, when the road's closed. That's when the only way back to town is by air. Where are you going with this?"

"There's one category that doesn't need approval. Emergencies. Now, there are two of these that occurred when Mr Felix was at the island, considering purchasing it. Both are medical emergencies – staff injuries, or so it says. But after those, when Mr Felix purchased the resort, emergencies became an almost weekly occurrence. Each one required both a helicopter and a vehicle, unlike the medical emergencies, which were just flights. This is exactly the same time as the bulk alcohol orders started." Phuong drew in a deep breath.

Emergencies. Shou the helicopter pilot had talked about emergency flights, and how they had to be kept quiet. No, secret. And everyone was hiding something…

"Meier," Xan blurted out. "I knew he was hiding something! But what did he do with all that alcohol? I can't see him drinking cheap beer and cask wine by the case. The only people who drink that would have to be desperate…bloody hell. He's the one who's been supplying illegal alcohol to the dry communities. Burgess and Nelson have been trying to work it out for months. That bastard!" She turned thoughtful. "But what about the rum? He wouldn't sell the good stuff…did the orders stop when he left?"

Jay coughed. "Um…I sort of…appropriated this month's case of rum. It was sitting there on your veranda. I was walking past on my way back from the library, and you'd just told me I had a guest…so I grabbed it. Figured you'd have noticed, but you never said anything. I still have most of it left. I only drank two bottles."

Xan made a note to cancel the rum order and get Jackie, the maid who cleaned Jay's villa, to bring the remaining bottles back to her house. The last thing she needed was him getting drunk and making a mess in the public areas again. Though he hadn't done that since Phuong arrived. Maybe the girl was stronger than she looked, if she could curb his drinking problem.

Phuong delicately cleared her throat. "I think you'll find that if you take out those suspicious expenses, the resort's bottom line looks quite favourable in the current economic climate, particularly in this region."

"And who are you, who knows so much about hotel finances? I don't remember your name on the payroll, or the list of new staff. What are your qualifications?" Jo demanded.

Phuong visibly shrank. "Nothing. I'm…no one," she mumbled.

Xan opened her mouth, ready to defend the girl who'd solved her mystery.

Jason beat her to it, jumping to his feet. "She's got more

experience managing hotel finances than any of the rest of us, though in Singapore and Vietnam, not here. She's in her final year of a business degree, and she's my wife. So be nice. Phuong, this is my sister, Joanne. Jo, meet my wife."

On the screen, Jo's eyes widened. "Your wife? You got married and I wasn't invited to the wedding? Well." She produced a bland smile. "Congratulations."

Silence entered the meeting room, stretching interminably.

Xan broke it. "If that's the financial statements dealt with, let's move on to my business plan for the resort."

Her phone beeped and she glanced down at the screen. Jo had sent her a message, asking for Phuong's full name and everything she knew about her. Xan nodded for Jo's benefit, before she launched into her carefully rehearsed speech about day trips, building relationships with local tour companies, and a video advertising campaign.

This was her hotel now. Her predecessor might have been a dodgy dick, but that was no reason not to let the resort shine in the brightest light. Especially if its owner was now married to an asset to the hotel who understood business management as well as Xan did.

The future looked rosy…and it wasn't even sunset yet.

FIFTY-ONE

"We should celebrate," Xan said after she'd terminated the call with Jo. "Your wedding and Phuong's financial detective work and drinking to the future of your hotel." She had a slight fixed quality to her smile, as if it pained her. "I'll go see if there's any champagne. And before you ask, yes, I'm paying for it." She left the meeting room.

"You were awesome, baby." Jason pulled Phuong into his lap and kissed her soundly. "We should celebrate, but I can think of better ways without wine." He dropped his voice to a whisper. "Sex on the beach. How 'bout it, baby?"

Déjà vu – Norman all over again. "I've never thought of sex as a good way to celebrate," Phuong protested weakly.

"That's because you've never had it with me, baby. Now, let's head down to the beach, so I can show you what I can do."

"No." She surprised Jason, but she'd surprised herself,

too.

"You've changed your mind? You seemed pretty sure of yourself in that shower." Jason rose and she slid off his lap. "But if you say so, we'll wait. Come for a walk on the beach with me instead? Just in case seeing it makes you change your mind again."

Phuong found her voice. "No, it's not that. I want…I'd like to do it inside. Without crabs. You promised you'd save me from them. So…inside, please."

"Inside?" Jason wrapped his arms around her and dipped her so that her shoulders touched the tabletop. "We could do it right here, if you like." He leaned over to kiss her, edging one thigh between hers so she could feel the heat of him through her knickers. His hands roamed over her body, opening another bottle of champagne inside her. Oh, yes…

"Bloody hell! Get a room, you two!"

Phuong stiffened at the sight of Xan's shocked face.

Jason helped Phuong to her feet. "You know what? We will." He snatched a piece of ice from Xan's ice bucket and popped it into his mouth before he slipped an arm around Phuong's waist. "C'mon, baby."

They made it into the house before Jason pressed her up against the wall, kissing her as if his life depended on it. "You're going to call the shots, baby. If we do this, it's how you want to," he said between kisses.

"I don't know where to start," she admitted.

"Getting our clothes off, maybe? Want me to undress you, or do you have a striptease in mind?"

She laughed. "No. Okay. As long as you don't rip my clothes off, you do it."

He grinned. "No ripping. Yes, ma'am. I'll take it slow. You'll see." He kissed her lips, before blazing a trail of kisses down her neck and across her shoulder, down her collarbone to the neckline of her dress. She was aware of her zip purring against her back as Jason released her from her dress, easing it slowly down her body as he kissed his way from her throat to her bra. He discarded the dress, letting it pool at her feet like desire was doing inside her.

Jason pulled her in close, his arms encircling her, before he unfastened her bra. He kissed her breast while his thumbs circled her nipples, inciting a protest from between her thighs as other parts of her ached for their turn in his expert hands.

Phuong fumbled with her knickers, sliding them over her hips. She let them drop to the floor as Jason spiralled kisses around her breasts. Each kiss sparked a response deep inside her, like she'd swallowed a whole box of new year firecrackers. He ignited them one by one, getting closer and closer to detonating the mortar in her middle.

It felt so good.

Without the wall and Jason holding her upright, she'd have melted into a gooey puddle on the floor.

"Do you want more, baby? Maybe me inside you?"

Yes! She mumbled a response that Jason somehow translated okay, because the next thing she felt was something hot between her thighs that he thrust inside her.

Phuong clenched her core in panic, expecting pain that never came.

"Just my fingers, baby, making you ready for more. You can keep holding tight to them like that, if you like, but if you ease up a little, I can work my magic on you again." He kissed her and wiggled his fingers inside her, setting off a cache of firecrackers she hadn't even known about. "Oh, you like that, don't you, baby?"

Her knees liquefied, so the only things holding her up were Jason's hand between her thighs and his chest pinning hers to the wall. No, holding her down, she realised as Jason lit that final firework. She soared, spiralling upwards into darkness. She didn't come down for several seconds, with her throat raw from screaming his name.

"Baby, tell me where you want me. Because you're so ready, and if you don't, our first time is going to be right here against this wall." He ground his groin against her so that hard ridge — huge, hot, hard ridge, she corrected herself nervously — in his pants pressed for entry to her core.

Come on in, she wanted to say. She blinked, her body flooded with such heady desire that she couldn't think straight.

"Phuong?" Jason asked in concern, moving away. Phuong started to slide down the wall as her traitorous legs failed. He caught her before she made it to the floor. "Not the wall, then. Maybe the bed. Wrap your legs around me. I'll carry you, baby."

His hands slid under her bum and lifted. His hands felt so good…and him between her thighs…

Phuong fastened her legs around his hips, rubbing herself against the rough fabric of his shorts, hoping, no, needing to reach the hardness underneath.

"Fuck, baby," he groaned, walking slowly as he carried her to…where, again?

She didn't care. Nothing mattered except his body and hers, tightly entwined and never letting go.

He sat, setting her on his firm thighs. Jason was as naked as she was now, and his…cock sat between them, pointed right at where she wanted it to be. She slid forward on his lap, aching to feel her flesh yielding to him completely.

His hand splayed across her belly. "Just a sec, baby." Foil crackled. He sheathed his cock in a slick, red condom. "Now I'm ready to dance. What's your favourite position, baby?"

"Wrapped around you, while you're deep inside me," she blurted out. "Jason, I need…I need… I don't know what I'm doing, but I need…"

"Shhh, you're my wife. It's my job to give you everything you need." His hands fastened around her bum again. This time, he pushed her forward until the head of his cock pierced the lips of her pussy. "Ready, baby?"

"Yes." She wasn't, not really. She'd never be ready for the sensation of something so large invading, overwhelming, conquering her from the inside out, but it felt so right. "You're home, baby," she said, shifting her hips and opening her legs wider as her body adjusted to Jason being a part of her.

He laughed gently. "You said it." He placed his hands on her hips. "You right there, baby? You feel so fucking good, wrapped so tight around me, I want to move, and make you scream my name again."

"Please," she begged.

One slow thrust, then another, as if he was testing her depths. Warm and waiting for him – why was he hesitating? Phuong tried to push him in deeper, to increase the pace on her own, but his hold on her hips tightened.

"Oh, we're doing this slow, baby. We've got happily for ever after here, so I'm taking my time with you." Laughing honey eyes captured hers and she surrendered with a kiss.

His cock....his cock…steadily pounding into her, driving thoughts of anything else out of her head as her climax built and built but didn't blow up like all the others had. She moaned and writhed, but he kept up his relentless pace, regular as a heartbeat, as he lit the charge on what wasn't a firework after all but a missile. A missile that blew her to bits around him, bliss that went on and on.

Jason held tight to her until she got her breath back into lungs she barely realised she still had. "Was it good for you, baby? Fairy tale quality?"

She laughed. "Definitely a happy ending. An incredible, amazing, mind-blowingly joyous ending."

Jason looked offended. "There's no fucking ending here, baby. Happily ever after, remember. I'm not finished with you yet. After that performance, I don't think I ever will be. Our own personal fucking fairy tale."

The story continues in
The Rock Star's Virginity

ABOUT THE AUTHOR

Demelza Carlton has always loved the ocean, but on her first snorkelling trip she found she was afraid of fish.

She has since swum with sea lions, sharks and sea cucumbers and stood on spray drenched cliffs over a seething sea as a seven-metre cyclonic swell surged in, shattering a shipwreck below.

Demelza now lives in Perth, Western Australia, the shark attack capital of the world.

The *Ocean's Gift* series was her first foray into fiction, followed by her suspense thriller *Nightmares* trilogy. She swears the *Mel Goes to Hell* series ambushed her on a crowded train and wouldn't leave her alone.

Want to know more? You can follow Demelza on Facebook, Twitter, YouTube or her website, Demelza Carlton's Place at:

www.demelzacarlton.com

Books by Demelza Carlton

Ocean's Gift series
Ocean's Gift (#1)
Ocean's Infiltrator (#2)
Ocean's Depths (#3)
Water and Fire

Turbulence and Triumph series
Ocean's Justice (#1)
Ocean's Trial (#2)
Ocean's Triumph (#3)
Ocean's Ride (#4)
Ocean's Cage (#5)
Ocean's Birth (#6)
How To Catch Crabs

Nightmares Trilogy
Nightmares of Caitlin Lockyer (#1)
Necessary Evil of Nathan Miller (#2)
Afterlife of Alana Miller (#3)

Mel Goes to Hell series
Welcome to Hell (#1)
See You in Hell (#2)
Mel Goes to Hell (#3)
To Hell and Back (#4)
The Holiday From Hell (#5)
All Hell Breaks Loose (#6)